THE HIDDEN SUMMER

THE HIDDEN SUMMER

GIN PHILLIPS

Dial Books for Young Readers

An imprint of Penguin Group (USA) Inc.

DIAL BOOKS FOR YOUNG READERS
A division of Penguin Young Readers Group
Published by the Penguin Group
Penguin Group (USA) Inc., 375 Hudson Street, New York, New York 10014, USA

USA / Canada / UK / Ireland / Australia / New Zealand / India / South Africa / China
Penguin Books Ltd, Registered Offices: 80 Strand, London WC2R 0RL, England
For more information about the Penguin Group visit penguin.com

Library of Congress Cataloging-in-Publication Data
Phillips, Gin.
The hidden summer / a novel by Gin Phillips.
p. cm.
Summary: When twelve-year-old Nell and her best friend, Lydia, are forbidden to see each other,
they hatch a plan to spend their summer days in an abandoned miniature golf course,
where they soon find others in search of a home.
ISBN 978-0-8037-3836-2 (hardcover)
[1. Best friends—Fiction. 2. Friendship—Fiction. 3. Mothers and daughters—Fiction.
4. Family problems—Fiction. 5. Homeless persons—Fiction. 6. Alabama—Fiction.] I. Title.
PZ7.P535Hid 2013
[Fic]—dc23
2012034033

Printed in USA   First Edition
1 3 5 7 9 10 8 6 4 2
Designed by Jasmin Rubero

The publisher does not have any control over and does not assume
any responsibility for author or third-party websites or their content.

To Laughlin, Liza, and Eli.
The putt-putt course is for you.

CHAPTER 1
THE TASTE OF HONEYSUCKLE

Behind our apartment building, past the chain-link fence, there's a dead tree that somehow hasn't fallen yet. It's standing up tall and straight, pretending to still be alive. Or maybe it's just scared to fall down—it's surrounded by briars and poison ivy and all sorts of weeds. It looks like nobody's set foot near that tree for a hundred years. Except for me and Lydia.

I like that the tree is an undiscovered place. I also like the honeysuckle, which grows in clumps of twisted, looping vines with delicate yellow and white blooms. They smell like honey tastes. Over time the honeysuckle has taken over the stumps and the shrubs and even the dead tree. Lydia and I stomp our way through the briars to get to the tree, and we sit on its roots, which stick out of the ground like the humps of sea monsters. We look up and it's a honeysuckle sky, little bits of blue showing through the vines. The honeysuckle is over us and around us—it falls down like curtains and hides us. We drink up the flowers sip by sip.

Today was the last day of school, and it's getting close to

sunset. We can hardly see each other—it's all shadows under the tree. I don't need light to talk to Lydia, though—she's my best friend and I can see her face even with my eyes closed.

"Mrs. Hughey definitely dyes her hair," she says, pinching the end off a honeysuckle blossom. "Amanda Elliot saw the roots when she was standing at Mrs. Hughey's desk."

Mrs. Hughey is the sixth-grade math teacher. We've always suspected her hair isn't naturally possible. It's the color of mustard.

"I heard Adam can do four one-armed push-ups," I say. I pull on the string of my own honeysuckle, taking my time, waiting for the little droplet to bead at the end of the flower. I hold it up to my mouth and let the liquid drop on my tongue.

Any and all things related to Adam Cooper are of interest to us. He's in seventh grade—one grade ahead of us—and, so far, has never actually spoken to either one of us. (The one boy who does speak to me plenty is named Gabriel Johnson. He has two parts in his very curly hair, so he has a puff of hair on the left, a puff in the middle, and a puff on the right. He looks slightly like a poodle. He writes me poetry, and I wish he'd stop.)

"Can you do a one-armed push-up?" Lydia asks.

I don't know. I've never tried. We both try to arrange ourselves on the dirt and roots and give the push-ups a shot, but neither of us can quite manage it. I can do one on my knees, but I'm pretty sure that's cheating. Eventually we just collapse on our bellies, propped on our elbows, and catch our breaths. The air smells like dirt and grass and honeysuckle.

"I have to tell you something," Lydia says as she rises,

brushing dead leaves off her stomach. She looks serious.

"You have to go to camp again this summer?" I guess. Last summer she got sent to an art camp in Tennessee for a whole month. Her mother loves camps.

"Worse," she says, picking at a leaf. Tearing a leaf to shreds, really. And she's got a piece of her hair in her mouth. She does that when she's nervous. Her hair is dark brown and long, but it's also usually got dried spit in it.

"Okay," I say, nervous myself now. She could be moving to another city. She could be sick. All of a sudden there's a bitter taste in my mouth that's nothing like honeysuckle.

Lydia's looking at me like she doesn't know how to finish what she started. I stare back at her. Her father is from Guatemala, and she has his lovely brown skin, but she has her mother's green eyes. I have freckles and light brown hair that's hardly any color at all.

"Nell," Lydia says, "my mother says we can't see each other for a little while."

I frown. It doesn't make sense. "Why? Why would she say that?"

"Your mom."

This could mean a lot of things. But Lydia's mother has known my mother for years, and Mom hasn't changed any in the last few days as far as I can see.

Lydia's chewing her hair with a lot of enthusiasm now. "Something . . . happened. I'm not sure what. My mom said she'd put up with your mom long enough, and she didn't think I should, um, like, hang around with you."

I don't know what to say to that.

"She also said we spend so much time together that neither of us get to have other friends. She said it would be better for us to get a little space."

"That's stupid," I say.

"I know," she says.

"How long is this break supposed to be?"

"She said for a couple of months. Or so."

"Two months is the whole summer! And what's 'or so' mean? That could be forever."

"We can still figure out how to see each other," says Lydia. "You know we can. I'll sneak out and come over. Otherwise what good is the back staircase for?"

She smiles, and I know she wants me to smile back. To see this as some big adventure. But I can't. I'm all for adventures, but Lydia has always been part of them.

Even if we sneak out, it means I can't go to Lydia's house. No more eating lunch at her kitchen counter, no more spending the night, no more throwing water balloons off her balcony or dressing up her dog in her mom's old nightgowns. We always stay at her house. Some of our best times have been after everyone else has gone to bed, whispering all our best secrets. That's when you really know you're best friends with someone, I think—when the entire world is asleep and there's no one left but the two of you and you can say all the things you're afraid to tell anyone else.

Now we'll hardly see each other this summer. Maybe not at all.

"Okay," I say, not looking at her.

"I'll let Mom calm down some and then ask her again. In a week or two."

"You better go home now," I say.

"Yeah, we should go," she says, and starts to stand up. I don't move.

"You go on," I say.

I don't know why I say it. It hurts her feelings. Her hands fall to her sides and flop around like fish out of water.

"You know I hate this, too," she says.

"I know," I say, because it's what I'm supposed to say. I do know that she hates it. But it's different for her. She's not the one who'll be alone in the apartment with my mother all summer. She'll have her nice bedroom and parents who don't pay much attention to her but never yell at her. Even though I love Lydia as much as I love anyone on this planet, for right now it all seems so unfair that I can barely keep the it's-okay-don't-worry-about-me smile on my face. And, trust me, I've had lots of practice keeping a smile on my face when I really don't feel like smiling.

Lydia waves at me and ducks under the honeysuckle curtain. I hate the sight of her leaving. But it hurts worse to see her next to me, like everything's normal, when I know it won't last.

Lydia's not the kind of friend you can replace. We've known each other since we were five, and she knows everything about me. I have nearly thirteen years worth of stuff that I'd have to explain to a new friend, and the thought of all that work is exhausting. Plus there are probably hundreds of inside jokes that are funny to me and Lydia and not anybody else. But, more than that, Lydia is never boring. She doesn't want to just sit in front of the television or fix her hair or read a magazine, which is more than I can say for plenty of girls in our class. She'll play volleyball and try back handsprings and watch horror movies. She's not afraid of anything. She will climb a tree no matter how tall. She will walk right up to a slobbering, growling dog and growl right back at it (at least if it's on a leash). She's sort of ferocious. In a good way.

I watch her climb over the fence into my backyard, then slip into her own yard. There's a broken board in the fence between my apartment building and Lydia's house. I met Lydia at that fence. My parents had just gotten divorced, and Mom and I hadn't even unpacked the boxes in our apartment. I was wandering through weeds growing in the back lot, hoping maybe there was a swimming pool Mom hadn't told me about, and I heard a voice say from the fence, "You can tell poison ivy because it has three leaves together." And there was Lydia, her dark head sticking through the hole in the fence.

I stay by myself for a while, breathing in the warm, sweet air. I don't know if they have honeysuckle in places other than Alabama, but here it's the best part of summer. There's a downside, of course. By the time the honeysuckle gets here, the air is so thick you can't breathe. The heat presses down on you until you think you'll sink right into the asphalt. Two seconds after you leave the air-conditioning, you can hardly remember what it felt like to ever be cool. That's summer.

I walk as slowly as I can up the stairs to our apartment. I turn the knob, and the apartment is as dark as the hallway, except for a light under the bathroom door. As I close the front door, the bathroom door swings open, and I can see someone step out. The light is behind her, so she's just a dark shape, but I can tell she's already in her nightgown. She just stands there.

"Hi, Mom," I say.

§ CHAPTER 2 ℒ
INTRODUCING MY MOTHER

ᴖ

My mother doesn't answer me. She moves toward the sofa, turning on one dim lamp. It makes the room look slightly green. I take a step toward her, trying to read her mood. I keep my voice friendly.

"It's sort of dark in here," I say.

She shrugs in a way that might be good natured. I am an expert when it comes to reading my mother, but that doesn't mean I don't make mistakes. The trick is to tell when she's in a carnivore mood or an herbivore mood. (Carnivores have sharp teeth for biting. You shouldn't get too close. But herbivores never attack.) In her carnivore moods, Mom is usually moving—pacing or fidgeting, tapping her foot or drumming her fingers on her leg. A cozy seat on the couch makes me think she might be in the mood for a conversation.

"Mom, what happened with Lydia's mother?" I ask. "She said Lydia can't see me anymore."

She leans forward on the sofa in a way that makes me step back. "And you figure I did something to her?"

She's staring at the floor, and I know this is a mistake. But losing Lydia has left me desperate. And angry.

"I don't know," I say, frustration in my voice. "Did you do something?"

She stands up fast and I take two steps back, turning away from her. I'm headed for my bedroom, where I can lock the door and wait until she calms down. Then my head snaps back, hard—she's grabbed my hair. She holds tight, so I can't move. I try to look at her out of the corner of my eye, but it makes my head hurt worse. I don't feel angry anymore. I feel like one of those gazelles on the National Geographic Channel that looks up from a nice cool drink of river water and sees a lion staring back.

Escape, escape, escape, the gazelle-me thinks.

"If you speak to me like that again," Mom says, "I will rip the hair out of your head. Do you hear me?"

"Yes, ma'am."

She doesn't mean it. She's never actually ripped the hair out of my head. And she hardly ever touches me, period. Not to hug me, not to smooth the wrinkles out of a shirt, and not to yank my hair. It's a bad sign when she touches me. My mother has a quick temper. That's the perfect phrase for it— it's so fast you can't see it coming.

"And don't you smirk at me," she snaps.

"Yes, ma'am. I'm sorry."

I say this with no tone whatsoever. I am a salesclerk on the store intercom announcing a sale on Aisle Three. I am the person who takes your ticket at the movies and tells you to enjoy your show. One thing you learn when your mother has a quick temper is to keep calm and collected. Parents have all the power anyway. They control whether you leave the house and where you can go and who you can see. You can't lose your temper if you want to have the slightest chance of winning, even if they have the luxury of losing theirs. I should never have let my anger show in the first place, no matter how upset I was about Lydia. I know the rules better than that.

It's taken me my whole life to figure out how to deal with my mother, but the rules aren't really all that complicated. These are the most important ones: When Mom is in a carnivore mood, avoid her if possible. Disappear—in your room, in the backyard, to Lydia's. If you cannot avoid her, disappear inside your own head. Make your face a mask and hide behind it. Show her what she wants to see.

"I didn't mean to smirk," I say in my Aisle Three voice. "But Lydia's my best friend, and I don't want to spend the whole summer without being able to see her. I just wondered what happened."

Sometimes, when I keep calm, Mom starts to realize that I'm the one who sounds like an adult and she sounds like a toddler having a temper tantrum. It makes her uncomfortable. She doesn't apologize, but she'll back down. She'll stomp out of the room and pretend like she never wanted to talk to me anyway.

"You can be so hateful," she snarls at me now, pulling me closer.

Well, sometimes it doesn't matter how calm and friendly I am. Sometimes her temper is so loud inside her head that she can't even hear what I'm saying. It looks like this is one of those times.

One more try. I try to ignore the sharp sting of my scalp.

"Did Lydia's mom do something to you?" I ask, trying to sound sympathetic.

She lets go of my hair, then spins me around by my shoulders, bringing her face close to mine. Her eyes are red and her blond hair is mashed flat against her head like something stuck to the bottom of your shoe. Sometimes she can be pretty, but she's not right now.

"Just go to your room," she says, and lets go of me.

I don't argue. I'm nearly to my bedroom door when she speaks again.

"It wasn't my fault," she says. "She came over here because the branches from the crape myrtles are over her driveway. All those little buds are landing on her car and making a mess. Our landlord won't return her call. She asked if I would try to reach him."

So far this sounds believable. Lydia's mom is very into how things look. She refuses to leave the house without lipstick, and her purse always matches her shoes. She hates for her Honda to get dirty. And our landlord never returns phone calls.

My mother crosses her legs as she sits back on the couch. The blue polish on her toenails is flaking off. She has long, slim legs that look like a magazine ad for panty hose or razors. She always says she doesn't know where I got my short, stubby legs.

"She treated me like I was her secretary," she says, although that's not how it seems to me. "I told her that it's harder to deal with that sort of thing when you're single. If she had a husband at home, he could do the yard work."

This also sounds believable. Mom has a talent for sensing people's sore spots. Lydia's mom is not single. She has a husband—Lydia's dad. But he's gone a lot. Like for months at a time. Lydia's mom says he travels a lot for business, but she says it like there's a period after every word—He. Travels. A. Lot. For. Business. You can tell she does not want to talk about it. And, of course, without anyone every mentioning it, my mother would know that. She'd smell it like sharks smell blood in the water.

I can imagine Lydia's mom's face as she stormed away from our apartment. She wouldn't have said anything nasty to my mom. She would have stewed about it all the way home, probably talking under her breath. She talks to herself when she's angry.

"She did seem upset," says my mother, leaning back into the couch. She reaches for the remote control. "She seems very sensitive."

I hurry into my room, close the door behind me, and walk to my window. The top of a dark red sun is vanishing over the trees. The knees of my stubby legs are weak. I want to be sure she's done with me before I relax. Soon I'll curl up on the bed and lose myself in a book, and then my mother and Lydia's mother and our whole apartment will go away.

I've read plenty of books. I spend a lot of time trying to disappear at home, and I like to find some place where no one will find me, like under the honeysuckle or behind the basement stairs. When you tuck yourself into a small space and plan to spend a lot of time there waiting until it's safe to come out, it's nice to have a book.

One thing I notice is that in books, a lot of kids' parents are dead. Or they're missing or on vacation. If they are around, the parents are kind and wise and do things like braid your hair and play board games with you. In books, parents aren't bad unless they're stepparents. (That's not fair, in my opinion. I've had several stepparents, and some of them were very nice.) Real parents are nice to their kids.

That is not my experience.

I have a list of things I wish my mother had never said.

"I wish you had brown eyes instead of blue ones."

"Why don't you smile more?"

"How can you love your father as much as you love me?"

I don't know where she came up with that last one. I figure I love my parents exactly the same. Which is to say that I love them but don't really like them very much. My father lives a few miles away, and I see him every other weekend. He lives alone at the moment. Mom just keeps getting married. She's always crazy about them in the beginning, but they never last long. At the moment she's married to Lionel, who's pretty okay. He likes doing crosswords with me and he makes great waffles. But I'm not going to let myself like him too much—it's easier that way.

Lydia has been my friend through five total stepparents and I don't know how many boyfriends and girlfriends. Sometimes Dad forgets to pick me up on Fridays, and sometimes Mom won't even look at me when I walk through the door, but Lydia is always there. She always wants to see me. She is the one person who I knew would never leave, and now she's gone.

Or she might as well be.

I turn to my map wall. When you can't concentrate on a book, maps are another good way to vanish and pop up in another place. The wall across from my bed is covered in maps. I have a city map of Boston and a funny map of the Gulf Coast with pictures of crabs and ice-cream cones. I have an old map of Iceland with really strange names and pictures of sea monsters in the ocean.

My favorite is a map of Europe done in gold and silver. I like the names I haven't heard of and the images they paint in my head. The Adriatic Sea makes me think of turquoise water and snow-colored shells. I like the names of all the little islands around Greece: Kythnos, Ios, Mykonos. I picture them shaped like giants coming out of the sea. I imagine Naples has grapevines everywhere, that Istanbul is shiny and bright like Christmas tree ornaments, and that Paris smells like coffee and bread.

I hear the soft thuds of moths hitting my windowpane, and I look out at the sky. As much as I like thinking about other cities, I like Birmingham the best. Here's the thing: I may not like what goes on in our apartment very much, but I love living in my neighborhood. I bet it's as good as Paris or Istanbul or even Venice. We're in an old part of the city that used to be elegant and stylish. Some of the houses are like castles, with turrets and balconies and big marble columns. A lot of them have their roofs fallen in and ivy growing up the walls, and they make you think of fairy tales or ghost sto-ries, depending on your mood.

Our apartment building is more in the ghost story cate-gory. It's three stories tall and there are cracks in the plaster walls. Some people have balconies, but you wouldn't want to stand on them because they'd probably fall off the building. We have roaches the size of house cats, which could be okay if they actually ate the mice that sneak through the holes in the cabinets and the rotten spots in the staircase.

But all you have to do is look through my window, and you'd see what I love most about being here. Our honey-suckle spot is only the beginning. The honeysuckle and the dead tree are in a big wild expanse of undergrowth— a sea of weeds that are as high as my waist, plus vines and small trees and wildflowers and dead stumps. We call it the Wasteland, and it's between my yard and the golf course.

I mean an actual golf course, an old one that hasn't been used in years, and it's maybe a hundred feet from my back fence. It still has a wooden sign at the closed-off entrance: THE LODEMA GOLF COURSE AND TENNIS CLUB. Lydia's mom said the owners went bankrupt or something. It's an eighteen-hole course with a putt-putt course attached, the kind with big fake animals and windmills and mountains at the holes. From our apartment you can see the overgrown trees—wide strong oaks and puffy white Bradford pears and Christmassy rows of pine trees—and past the trees you can see the lights and skyscrapers of downtown Birmingham. In winter I can see the course itself, which still has the flags sticking up out of the holes. The grass is tall and shaggy, though—not at all like those golf courses you see on TV with grass like carpet. But the best thing about Lodema is that you can see the main attractions at the putt-putt course—there's a dried-up waterfall, some kind of tower, and the head and neck of an orange dinosaur. I call him Marvin. I named him after Stepfather No. 2, my favorite of the temporary dads.

You can appreciate it all from Lydia's house much better than mine, though. She's got the best views. And a balcony that won't fall off the house.

I look out my window at Marvin's tiny head and muscular neck, and I think how much I would like him to rise up, alive, and come pounding through the trees toward me. He'd smash our fence with one swipe of his tail. I'd lean out of my window and climb on his head, then I'd slide down his neck to his back. He'd carry me away back to the golf course, where I'd live happily ever after with dinosaurs and other plastic pets.

I can hear my mother banging pots in the other room. I wonder if she will remember that I haven't eaten any dinner.

Here's a warning: Don't go thinking that this story will end with my mother coming to her senses and realizing her mistakes and begging me to forgive her. She will not hug me and tell me she loves me. It's not going to happen. She isn't a bad person. She isn't evil. I think she just wishes I didn't exist.

CHAPTER 3
FAVORITE WORDS

The next day, I decide to visit my grandparents since Mom is still in a bad mood, and I haven't figured out how to see Lydia. I called her right after breakfast, and she picked up just long enough to whisper that she couldn't talk because her mom was home.

It's about a forty-five-minute walk to Memama and Grandpops's place, and the whole walk is along winding neighborhood streets. When it's not 90 degrees, it's pleasant. But now my shirt is stuck to my back, and my sweat mustache is dripping into my mouth. It's worth it, though, because I like seeing my grandparents. They like seeing me, too. In fact, I'm sure if they realized how bad it was at home, they'd ask me to come live with them.

But they really don't have much space, and I'm not sure kids are even allowed to live in the Beachhaven Retirement Center. (There is no beach, by the way. I've looked over the entire grounds, and I never found anything other than an empty bird fountain shaped like an oyster. I told Memama the name was false advertising. She told me that Across-from-the-Winn-Dixie Retirement Center did not have a very appealing ring to it.) Still, I like having them at the center—they're a lot closer than they were when they had their own house. Now I visit them almost every Tuesday afternoon, and, sometimes, like today, I go on days when I just can't stand to stay home.

My mother hates coming here to visit them—she says it smells like sick people. But I enjoy it. Everyone smiles and says hello to me, and several of the ladies like to hug me or pat my arm as I walk by. They don't smell sick to me. Mostly they smell like baby powder and perfume, and the thin skin on their hands is soft like flower petals. Along the hallway to my grandparents' apartment, I pass huge bouquets of lilies and carnations, gleaming mirrors, and, my favorite, a big glass cabinet full of live canaries.

I knock on the door and Memama answers—she wraps her arms around me and she kisses my cheek with a little smack. A wave of ice-cold air-conditioning washes over me. I smell something baking, something sweet. I'm betting on cookies.

"Hi, sugar," she says. "You look beautiful."

"Thanks," I say. Compliments make me uncomfortable.

She touches my cheek with her flower-petal fingertips and calls back to my grandfather, who's in the den. "Doesn't she have the most beautiful skin, George? She's just lovely."

"Skin like a gopher," he says.

Memama says Grandpops has a knack for unique phrases. Mostly he says things that don't make much sense. But they're usually interesting things.

I go and hug Grandpops in his recliner. He has a lot of

trouble standing, so usually he just sits. He likes to squeeze me until I make an *oof* sound. He always smells like fresh grass to me, even though he hasn't mowed a yard in years. He's got stubble that's pleasantly rough against my cheek.

"You feel like sandpaper," I say. It's what I always say.

"Trying to get the rough edges off you," he says. Which is what he always says.

I plop down on the sofa with a thump, look toward the kitchen, and wait.

"Ladies sit," Memama says almost immediately. "They don't collapse in a heap."

I smile and inhale the cookie smell again.

"I'm not a lady yet," I say.

Their apartment is filled with polished wooden furniture and rugs and blankets and pillows and candleholders and glass. Memama loves glass—she has bells and paperweights and colored flowers and birds sipping at nectar and a unicorn, and all of them catch the sunlight when it comes in through the window.

By the time she brings in cookies and lemonade, I've almost stopped sweating. I say thank you, bite into a snickerdoodle, and take my time licking the cinnamon and sugar off my lips.

Grandpops is as happy with the cookies as I am. "Tastes like leaves falling," he says.

We nod. Memama runs a hand through my hair, and I melt a little deeper into the sofa. Things that make me feel happy: cookies, fishing, a good book, Lydia, the touch of Memama's hand. Memama's big into touching. And I don't mind at all. I may not be all that comfortable with her saying I'm beautiful, or even with her saying "I love you"—that sort of talk makes me turn pink—but when I feel her hand soft against my hair, when she hugs me tight or presses her powdery cheek against mine, I feel beautiful and loved and all sorts of good things without her saying a word.

I close my eyes and enjoy my cookie.

"When did you learn how to make snickerdoodles, Memama?" I ask.

She wrinkles up her forehead and thinks. Her gray hair is curled tight like she's had a permanent recently, and everything about her from her chin to her earlobes is delicate.

"I guess I learned from my mother," she says. "Or . . . wait. I think I had them for the first time on a picnic. A friend's mother made them, and I asked for the recipe."

"How old were you?" I ask.

I love it when Grandpops and Memama tell me stories while I'm curled up on the couch with the glass shining around me. I especially like it when they tell me about growing up. Both of them grew up in the country, although they were hundreds of miles away from each other. Memama's father worked in a steel mill, but he also had a little plot of land where they grew vegetables and raised chickens. Grandpops's dad owned hundreds of acres, a real giant farm with men he paid to work on it. They had horses and cows and cats that caught mice in the barn and big machines to make the dirt ready to plant.

It sounds nice, all that space.

They talk about growing up in the country; they talk about

how they couldn't get much sugar or meat during the Great Depression. They talk about riding on trains and how they used to sit around a radio at night instead of the television.

"I was in high school," says Memama. "It wasn't much of a picnic. There were several of us girls there, and we were picking apples mainly. It wasn't easy, either, trying to climb a tree in a dress and stockings."

I have trouble imagining Memama in a tree. But that's another good thing about their stories. They let me see Memama and Grandpops before I'd ever met them. If I look close now, I can see the young girl under my grandmother's face.

"Why did y'all want to pick apples?" I ask.

"For pies, of course. That tree had the best pie apples. Sweet and tart. We'd fill our skirts up with them and then dump them into buckets on the ground."

"Eating as you went," says Grandpops. "Like squirrels."

I look down at my lap. Squirrels make me think of the time Lydia tried to catch one for pet. The squirrel darted up a tree, and when Lydia dove to grab it, she ran straight into the tree like some scene out a cartoon. Usually that memory makes me smile. Now it doesn't, though. It reminds me of how different life will be without Lydia. And if just a mention of squirrels makes me think of Lydia, how many other random words will make me think of her?

Usually being with Memama and Grandpops helps me forget everything but stories and hugs and the smell of sugar. But I can't forget Lydia, not even here.

"By the time we got home, we wouldn't want to see another apple for quite a while," Memama is saying. "But that's what you can't understand now, Nell—you didn't go to the grocery store. You walked outside. Apples and plums and blackberries, vegetables from the garden, pecans and poke salad, and fish in the creek."

"We bathed in the creek," says Grandpops. "One time we found a dead cow floating upstream, and we waited about bathing in the creek for a while. But not too long."

"Oh, we bathed in the creek, too, of course," Memama says.

"I spent the night in the woods for a whole week once," says Grandpops. "Me and the rest of the boys shot birds with pellet guns and fished with worms we dug up. Cooked everything over the fire. You kids all spend too much time inside now. You don't know what it's like to get out and escape."

I almost tell him that "escape" is one my favorite words.

"The house was our parents' space," Memama says. "We didn't have the money to go to movies or restaurants, and there weren't any shopping malls. Our place was the woods or the creek or walking along the side of the road. You got out into the wide open space, and it made you feel free."

Another memory comes to me, and this one does make me smile. When I was younger, sometimes Memama and Grandpops would take me camping in their backyard. We'd bring sleeping bags into a tent, and they'd tell not-scary ghost stories. Memama would bring a Tupperware container of cookies with us, and Grandpops would bring an armload of pillows for me to lie on. When I needed to go to the bathroom, I could run into the house real quick—it was the best camping possible. And it was really the closest I'd gotten to wide open space.

Long after I've eaten my last snickerdoodle, I walk very slowly back to the apartment. I stop at a magnolia tree and bury my nose in a flower. I blow a few dandelions and watch the little parachutes drift off on the wind. I follow a trail of ants to a smashed caramel. Once—at Stepdad No. 3's house—Lydia and I followed a trail of ants from under the kitchen window, around the side of the house, over the brick wall, under the hydrangea bush, all the way to a dead stump in the neighbors' yard. It was maybe a quarter mile of single-file ants. That was during our experiment phase. We laid out a buffet for the ants to see which they liked the best—a Fig Newton, peanut butter, or a peppermint. The Fig Newton won. Around that same time, we tried to grow a tadpole into a frog, but we left the bucket out in the sun and the tadpole got cooked. We did a better job of turning a daisy pink by putting red food coloring in its water.

The experiments lasted a few weeks before we moved on to something else. That's what we do: we make discoveries. We learn things. Lydia and I are each other's escape routes. We take each other away from the old, unpleasant things—mothers with their weird silences and bad tempers and dads with their long absences—and we uncover new, incredible things. We know every cluster of honeysuckle in the neighborhood. We can hula-hoop and fly kites and name every kind of butterfly, and we both speak excellent Pig Latin. We came up with a pretty good mind-reading act. It started with me picturing different objects in my head, and she'd try to name the objects. Out of maybe two hundred tries, she guessed one right: pepperoni pizza. So I started imagining pepperoni pizza every time, and she started guessing pepperoni pizza every time. It was pretty impressive. (When I say that it was impressive, I really mean it was impressive to anyone who was under five years old.)

I lie in bed that night and think about all the things Lydia and I have seen and done. I miss her. If I'm honest, I also miss her house. It's nice to have someplace to go when you need to get out of your own house. I think about Memama and Grandpops splashing through water and climbing up trees. I think about escaping. I think about Marvin. I think about the one place Lydia and I haven't discovered yet.

That's when I figure out what I need to do. What Lydia and I need to do.

We need to move to the golf course.

CHAPTER 4

THE CHRISTOPHER COLUMBUSES OF GOLF

∿

"We can't move to the golf course," says Lydia.

We're talking softly so that in case her mother gets home early from work, we'll hear the car door slam.

"Sure we can," I say. "I mean, we'd still have to come home at night, but it could be our own secret place during the day. A place for just us."

I'm not surprised she finds the idea less appealing than I do. We're sprawled across her soft bed with its puffy light blue duvet on it—I didn't even know the word "duvet" before I spent the night with Lydia for the first time. She has a chair covered in fake zebra skin. Her beige carpet is so soft you want to make snow angels on it, and she has a shiny beaded curtain hanging from her doorway. Everything in her room makes you want to touch it. (That includes her dog, Saban, who is a white puffball with eyes.)

The golf course would be a serious step down for her, bedroom-wise.

I usually think of Lydia as being braver than me. She'll always jump into the pool first, even if we haven't tested the water. She'll knock on anyone's door, even if she doesn't know them. (That came in handy during the summer that we tried to learn how to throw a boomerang. That boomerang landed in a lot of different backyards.) But going to the golf course isn't just about bravery. It's about wanting to escape. And I want to escape much more than Lydia does.

Lydia flops on her back and stares at the stars on her ceiling.

"What will we eat?" she asks. "What would we do? Where will we shower or go to the bathroom?"

"We could have our days free to do whatever we want," I say. "No moms. No checking in with anyone."

"No air-conditioning," she says.

"No rules," I say.

Saban sneezes twice and start licking himself. Lydia looks skeptical.

"What do you want, really?" she asks. "To run away?"

I snort. "Of course not. I'm not an idiot."

The flaw with most running-away plans is that you have to stop going to school. That may be fun in the short term, but what are you going to do in a year or two or three? When you're ready to start learning how to be a film director or an astronaut or a veterinarian? You need school for that. But you'll have given up school—you'll be wandering the streets or waiting tables or sweeping floors.

I don't just want to escape for a little while—I want to escape for forever.

Lydia and I ran away once before, when we were ten. We got as far as the Chevron station at the bottom of the hill. We'd planned to stock up on snacks and drinks, then we were going to walk to the YMCA, which we knew would give you a bed if you needed one. (Since then I've learned that we should probably have gone to the YWCA, because it's for women.) Anyway, Lydia's mom drove past us and pulled over and offered us milk and Rice Krispies Treats if we'd come home. Lydia's mom has some issues, but stupidity is not one of them. We were not strong enough to resist marshmallow.

I think that I'm steadier now. I think that sweets would not be enough to make me come back.

"Do you want to stay here?" I ask her, looking around at her perfect room. "If you do, just tell me."

She looks at me and pulls her hair out of her mouth.

"No," she says. "You know I don't want to stay here. Not if you're not here. When you're here, I don't mind Mom. Without you, it's so . . . well, Saban's not very good at conversation."

She pets her dog's head apologetically, but Saban doesn't seem insulted.

There are times when the thing I most want in the world is for my mother to stop noticing me. But Lydia's mother never notices her, and it does not seem to be a good thing. Actually, Lydia's mom is sort of like the rest of the house—she looks perfect. Not perfect as in beautiful, but perfect as in *exactly* what a mom should look like. Sweet and smiling and cuddly. She cooks delicious things and has fresh flowers on the table, and when she picks Lydia up from school, she hugs her and kisses the top of her head. I used to be really jealous. But then I realized that those things are mostly for looks. Lydia's mom spends most of her time watching TV in her bedroom or out shopping and visiting friends. She's gives Lydia compliments and leaves her cupcakes and chocolate chip cookies on the kitchen counter, but sometimes Lydia goes days without her mom saying more than "good morning" and "good night" to her. They don't talk much.

"I just don't want to leave if we're only going to be dragged back with things even worse than they were before," Lydia says. "If we're doing this, I want to make sure we're doing it right."

"So what else do you want to know?" I ask.

"How will we keep our mothers from noticing we're gone? Why would they let us disappear every day? And how do we even know we'd like the golf course?"

The thing about Lydia's questions is that she's not being difficult. She's not looking for an excuse to say no. She's assessing the plan, trying to find the holes in it. Before she decides to do anything, she likes to know what she's getting into. She's someone who would never have gotten on the *Titanic* before counting all the life rafts.

Lydia pops her hair back in her mouth, but I interrupt before she can comment on Marvin. "Just come with me tonight," I say. "Just once. Let's see what's out there, and we'll decide if it could work."

She stares at the ceiling a second, rolls over on her stomach, and then she smiles. I know I've won.

"You think it'll turn out better than last time?" she asks.

We'd tried to explore the golf course a couple of years ago, but it didn't go very well. It hadn't looked like it would be that hard—all we had to do was climb a five-foot chain-link fence. We'd climbed fences that high plenty of times. We went at the same time, racing over the fence. But some of the wire was rusted, and as we swung our legs over the top, a stray bit of chain link cut Lydia's ankle. She had to go get a tetanus shot.

We hear a car door, and I'm off Lydia's bed and headed toward the hallway before she even opens her mouth. I nearly trip over Saban, who apparently thinks he's going with me.

"Meet me under the honeysuckle at eleven o'clock tonight," I say. "No flashlights."

I do not want to run into Lydia's mother. I have a feeling she would not seem so sweet and cuddly if she found me in her house right now. Actually, I'm not sure she's ever spoken to me beyond "don't slam the front door." Barring me from the house would make more sense if it had seemed like she'd ever noticed I was *in* her house in the first place.

I hear Lydia's voice just as I open her mother's bedroom door.

"Make it eleven thirty," she says. "My mom will go to bed at eleven P.M. after *Supermodels in a Submarine* is over. The mosquito trucks have been driving by between eleven and eleven thirty every night. They make enough noise that I can get down the stairs and out the front door without her hearing me."

This is another reason Lydia and I work well as friends— I like words and she likes numbers. She's very good at schedules and budgets and math tests. I close her mother's bedroom door quietly, then slip out the sliding glass door to the balcony and jog down the outside staircase.

That night I slip out of our apartment at eleven fifteen,

just to make sure Lydia doesn't have to wait on me. I don't want to give her a chance to change her mind. The front door creaks too loudly, so I climb through my window until I'm sitting on the outside of the windowsill. A tree limb comes within a foot of the window, so I swing one leg and then the other over the limb. (I worry about roaches, which an exterminator once told me live in trees, but I can't see any.) I scoot along the branch until I can jump down onto the fire escape coming off Mrs. Woodard's kitchen. From there it's easy.

It's a crescent moon tonight, but it's a bright one. I can see the lights of the city past the golf course—the fire red letters of the City Federal Building, the dark column that's Alabama Power, and the balls at the top of the Harbert Building. I try to focus on my feet, taking tiny steps and feeling for any sudden dips in the ground. I wonder if snakes sleep at night and whether they sleep on top of the ground or deep in holes. I'm hoping for deep holes. I'm nearly to the honeysuckle tree when I hear other footsteps.

"Nell?"

I flash my cell phone at Lydia. It's not as noticeable as a flashlight, but it's enough to see by. It's not the only thing I've brought with me—I have a backpack with a blanket, a bottle of water, a couple of pieces of paper, and a Swiss army knife that Marvin (the stepdad, not the dinosaur) gave me. I've given some thought to where we should climb over the fence. There's an old gate with a padlock on the Highland Avenue side, but we'd have to walk half a mile to get to the gate. Instead I've decided we should climb across right behind my apartment building.

We've both worn jeans and tennis shoes instead of shorts and sandals—in the years since the course has been abandoned, the plants have taken over. There's no telling how much poison ivy or thorns there might be back there. We clomp through the weeds of the Wasteland until we get to the fence, and the only thing we can see other than the fence is tall clumps of pampas grass. It looks sort of like pussy willows at the top, with soft feathery plumes, but the grass itself will slice your skin open if you touch it wrong. It's growing along the fence, and it's just as dangerous as the rusted bits of metal.

"You ready?" I ask.

Lydia nods and reaches one hand toward the fence.

"Wait," I say. I dig through my backpack and pull out the blanket.

"You cold?" Lydia asks.

I answer her by tossing the blanket on to the fence, hoping it'll protect our hands and feet. "I'll go first," I say.

I wedge the toes of my tennis shoes in the fence holes, and the wire bites into my fingers as I climb. When I get to the top, the pampas grass makes it impossible to jump straight down. I take my time and get balanced on the top of the fence, with the arch of my foot curved around the metal bar. Then I raise my other foot so that for a couple of seconds I'm squatting on top of the fence, frog-like. I take a breath and launch myself up and out. I clear the pampas grass other than my little finger, which stings as it brushes against a long leaf. I'm hurtling forward, not seeing anything, and then I land hard, collapsing into a pile. Long grass tickles my nose.

I check for blood on my finger—it's not too bad—as Lydia makes her way up the fence. As soon as she's landed, we brush ourselves off and start moving forward. The underbrush is thick, and it's hard to see anything, even with the light from my cell phone. The grass behind us blocks out any light from the houses and the streetlights. Little saplings are all around us, and we use them for handholds as we push our way through the weeds and vines. Finally we're in a clearing, with no tangles of plants around our feet. There's nothing but tall grass.

We take in the view. At first it's not much. It's dark and the sky with its bright moon and few stars is more eye-catching than anything around us. But as we stand there, our eyes sharpen. I can tell this must have been a fairway—it's long and flat. I think I see the shine of a lake in the distance.

I wonder how many snakes are in this grass.

"What are the four deadly poisonous snakes in Alabama?" I ask Lydia.

"Shut up, Nell."

I answer myself silently. We learned them in fourth grade: copperhead, cottonmouth, rattlesnake, coral snake. Once I watched a slow-motion video of a rattlesnake killing a bird— the snake moved so fast that the bird couldn't even fly away. It just sat there and let the snake sink its fangs into its feathery little body.

I am beginning to wish I didn't watch so much National Geographic.

Still, for all we know, this golf course has turned into the lost city of snakes since people stopped coming here. I saw a movie about a snake—it had old crumbling ruins full of human skulls, and snakes were crawling in and out of their eye sockets. There's also the possibility—especially in the dark—of falling into a big pit full of snakes just waiting for a snack.

I am beginning to think I should just stop watching television altogether.

I focus on the sound of our feet moving through the grass. *Swishhhh crunch. Swishhhh crunch.* Snakes make *swish*ing sounds, too, it occurs to me.

"I was thinking that maybe we should live downtown," Lydia says.

I wonder if she could tell that I needed distracting. This is one of our favorite topics—what we'll do when we grow up. We'll be roommates, of course.

"We could get a loft," she continues. "My aunt has one. We could get one with high ceilings and brick walls. And wood floors. And a big couch where we can watch movies at night."

While she talks, we keep heading in a straight line, using the red letters of the City Federal Building as a compass point. As long as we head toward it, we won't get lost. Everything looks the same. There's just grass and occasionally a tree, and I think I might have seen a lake off to our left. The sounds are more noticeable than any of the sights. The crickets are playing their little legs like violins—*reek-eek, reek-eek*—and the bullfrogs are croaking out their own rhythm. There's the howl of coyotes nearby. Very nearby. I shiver. At least the howling takes my mind off snakes.

We live at the bottom of Red Mountain, which was named for the color of the iron they used to mine out of the mountain. They stopped mining a long time ago, so now there are boarded-up mines—strewn in the middle of all the nice neighborhoods—that haven't been used in sixty or seventy years. I've always heard rumors that coyotes live in the abandoned mines. Sometimes you'll hear a neighbor say they saw one through their window, slinking across the street in the middle of the night. If a yappy dog goes missing, usually people blame it on coyotes. (I personally think it's a very long list of suspects if you're asking who would want to get rid of that Pomeranian that used to bark at leaves falling.)

We stand for a minute, listening to the howls. A few neighborhood dogs bark back. Then, from right next to me, comes the loudest howl of all.

"Ah-ooooooooh," howls Lydia, her face tilted up to the sky. *"Ah-ah-oooooooh!"*

"What are you doing?"

"I'm saying hello," she says. "And I'm saying it's a nice night for hunting mice."

I giggle. "Do coyotes hunt mice?"

She pauses and cocks her head to the side. There's another howl or two in the distance. "Oh, yes," Lydia translates. "They say mice are delicious. They taste like hot dogs."

"Well, tell them to stay off the golf course tonight. They might think we taste like hot dogs."

She doesn't howl much longer, and then we both just settle into the stillness. I look up at Red Mountain and there are a few houses still lit up, but mostly just streetlights. None of the sounds we hear are human. There are no voices, not even any cars. The wind blows past us, and it feels like we've just landed on a new planet. All of a sudden I don't worry about snakes or coyotes or anything creeping around in the dark. All I can think about, as the wind lifts up my hair, is that anything is possible out here. You know that feeling you get when you have a nice brand-new set of colored pencils, you pull out a sketch pad, and you just stare at that blank page for a minute? Because there's a kind of rush knowing you can draw anything, create anything—that snow-white page is just waiting to be filled.

Standing on the golf course is like that feeling, only way, way bigger.

"I wonder if this is how Christopher Columbus felt," I say.

"I think he explored America during the daylight," says Lydia.

I see Marvin over the trees, and the dark seems a little less dark. Everything seems a little more familiar.

"Let's go see the putt-putt course," I say.

CHAPTER 5

HERE BE MONSTERS AND ROCKET SHIPS

The putt-putt course is like nothing I've ever seen. Unlike the real golf course, the grass is fake here, so it looks a lot like it must have when it was still working. Everywhere we step is either concrete or green carpet. There are some standard things—Holes One, Two, and Three involve a windmill, a lighthouse, and a dry waterfall. But then things start to get interesting. On Hole Four, if you actually had a club and ball, you'd hit the ball through the legs of a zebra, and then it would roll around the curves of a giant sleeping python.

Hole Five is Marvin, and he looks even better up close. He's at least twelve feet tall—I can barely touch his huge chest. He's an orange brontosaurus with subtle splashes of purple, if purple can be subtle. He's smiling so you can see stubby little teeth and a pink tongue. He's like a cartoon come to life. I reach up and pat his belly, and it makes a surprisingly loud sound—there's a clang and an echo, like maybe Marvin is hollow. I walk around him slowly, running my hand along his short legs and his thick tail. When I come to his back leg,

I notice a crack in his skin, and I trace the crack until I realize it's a rectangle.

"I think this is a door," I say to Lydia.

"Of course," she says. "Everyone knows brontosauruses had doors in their back legs. That's where they stored their food for the winter."

Lydia can get a little sarcastic when she's tired.

I try to pry the leg-door open, but it won't budge. Finally I push it—a couple of light shoves and then a hard one—and it springs open with a whine. A lightbulb comes on inside.

"Everyone knows brontosauruses had lightbulbs inside their stomachs," says Lydia, but quietly. "Um, Nell, surely they turned off the electricity when this place closed down. I mean, didn't they?"

"I guess not."

"Could be ghosts," she says, sounding a little too excited for my tastes. Lydia loves horror movies.

"It's not ghosts," I say.

"Could be," she says, squinting at the open doorway. "Ooooh, like, maybe creepy golfer ghosts, floating around and dragging their clubs behind them."

Well, that image makes the idea of ghosts a little less scary. Still, I walk in slowly, just in case there's some long-lost janitor trapped in here. Or in case Lydia's right and a very weird ghost—golfer or not—has chosen to haunt the inside of a dinosaur. But there's nothing here, at least nothing alive. The light is soft and warm, not the kind that gives you a headache. The door must have been sealed tight, because we don't see any bugs or spiderwebs or birds' nests. What we do see are ribs and veins and a very large fake pink heart tucked in between fake pink lungs.

All around us, the inside of Marvin's body is pale and pink and crisscrossed by painted veins and arteries. It's actually very pretty—it makes the walls look fragile and delicate, like butterfly wings. Marvin's eyes are made out of some sort of screen, so when you look toward his head you can see the night sky through two eye-shaped holes.

I don't say so to Lydia yet, but I decide in a split second that I want to move into Marvin's rib cage. When you go to a summer camp, you stay in a cabin. Lydia's taught me that much. Marvin will be my cabin. I will cover his floor with blankets and pillows, and I'll close the door to keep out mosquitoes and roaches. I notice an electrical outlet, and I think a small Lava lamp would go really nicely with the veins and arteries.

"Better than we thought, huh?" I say, in an encouraging way.

"Yeah," she says slowly. "It's not bad."

I suspect she's still thinking about her comfortable bedroom, but I know I've got her attention when we get to Hole Six. It's a spaceship. Or maybe it's a rocket. I'm pretty sure it's what I thought was a tower from my bedroom window.

"Where do you think you're supposed to hit the ball?" Lydia asks.

I was wondering the same thing. Hole Six starts with a long, Z-shaped course, maybe a par 3, but there's no place for you to putt the ball. Instead of a hole at the end of the Z shape, there's this huge rocket ship. Maybe whoever designed it got so interested in building the rocket, they forgot about adding a hole for the ball. Really, now that I think about it, this whole putt-putt course feels like maybe somebody had a little too much fun designing it. I mean, Marvin has veins on the inside. He has pores on his skin. And he has toenails. That seems like more details than are actually necessary.

This rocket is nearly as tall as Marvin, and it also has a door. A pink light glows from underneath.

"Ghosts?" I say.

"We can hope," says Lydia with a grin, and she makes a dash for the door.

I follow right behind her, and the first thing we see is a control panel with blinking yellow and red lights. It's lit up like the flashing lights on a Christmas tree. (You can understand why the people who owned the golf course went out of business if they couldn't even remember to turn the lights out after they went bankrupt.) There are two chairs by the control panel, and we sit down in them for a little while and push buttons while we spin the chairs around. Then we head up the spiral staircase behind the chairs, which looks like it leads to some sort of loft.

"Do you think they built fake aliens up here?" asks Lydia as our feet thud on the staircase. "Who sleep in fake bunk beds?"

"Maybe fake astronauts?" I suggest. "Or maybe astronauts who have fake aliens bursting out of their chests?"

Like I said, Lydia's a horror movie nut, so she actually gets that joke.

There aren't any aliens at the top of the stairs. But there are bunk beds. And a steering wheel that looks like it belongs on an old ship instead of a rocket ship. The walls are mirrored, so I see at least twenty versions of myself and Lydia. There's a skylight at the top of the rocket and round windows everywhere you look. We're so high that we don't even see the trees—all we see are stars and sky and endless reflections of ourselves.

Lydia doesn't say anything, but I can see she's impressed.

"Like it?" I say.

She shrugs. She's still thinking things over, so it'll take her a little while to be able to actually say she's impressed. I can deal with that.

We check out the rest of the course. Hole Seven is a two-level hole with a slide—an actual slide—and it looks like you hit your ball down the slide, and it rolls out by the hole, and then you slide down after it. We try out the slide, but it's not very slick. We each get stuck about halfway down and have to scoot on our butts the rest of the way down. Hole Eight is a volcano—you'd aim for a hole in the base, and then it looks like the volcano would shoot your ball out of the top. We climb the fake rocks, peer into the open pit, and see the spring that would launch a ball.

Hole Nine is the most amazing. It looks simple at first— just a flat green with two little empty concrete ponds next to three openmouthed fish. A ball could roll into any of the three mouths. But on the other side of the fish, there's a staircase leading down into the ground. There's a soft glow coming from the bottom of the stairs, and, since we're used to how things work here by now, we jog down the stairs, expecting to see something strange and wonderful.

We're not disappointed. We wind up in a hallway, and the walls of the hallway are glass. Pretty soon we realize that they're not walls at all—they used to be aquariums. There's still algae in a few spots, plus lonely bits of colorful rocks and coral. We stop and peer through the glass.

"I bet there were sharks in here," Lydia says, drawing a circle with her finger on the dust-covered glass.

"It's not big enough for sharks."

"Small sharks. Small killer sharks."

I'd bet there were some jellyfish myself, plus maybe some eels and manta rays. But I do like the idea of sharks.

Lydia tugs at my shirt. "Look at that, Nell."

She's pointing to a bright green arrow that's been painted on the glass. It's right about eye level, and it slants down to the left. Next to the arrow is a group of solid purple circles—not in any order, just a bunch of round purple dots. Next to the dots are scattered blue marks, like eyebrows or sideways commas. The drawings remind me of cave paintings I've seen in books, but it seems very unlikely that prehistoric people were living in a putt-putt course. Also, the paint is shiny and new looking.

"Some other kids got in here and left some graffiti?" I suggest.

"It's weird graffiti," Lydia says. "There aren't any words in it."

The arrow doesn't seem to be pointing to anything, and there's no other writing on the glass. But Lydia loves a good puzzle, and she stands there for a while trying to solve the symbols.

"Go underground to find snow and rain?" she guesses. "Um, there are frog eggs and tadpoles in the basement? Or, wait, balls roll downhill and then they hit . . . worms?"

I thump her on the back of the head and she glares at me. But she stops talking.

About ten feet past us, at the end of the hallway, there's another staircase that leads us to ground level. We climb up and realize that the three fish mouths in the first part of the hole would spit out the golf balls next to the top of this staircase. The aquariums don't seem to have had anything to do with the route of the ball—they're just here for fun. Like the rocket ship.

Back in the night air at the end of Hole Nine, we look around us at the entire overwhelming putt-putt course, with its animals and machines and underground shark houses. I feel a twinge of sadness that this place is here, so magical and odd, and no one has been able to enjoy it for so long. It's such a waste. The crickets are chirping, and the shadows of the trees are waving across the fake grass. We didn't close any doors, so several of the holes are shining with faint lights. There's a glow all around us.

Sometimes when Mom goes out late at night, Lionel leaves on the kitchen light so that she can see it from her car when she gets home. He says that coming home to a dark home is lonely, but a lit-up window means someone is waiting for you. That's what it feels like here—like the golf course was leaving the lights on for us. And we've finally come home.

"Nell," says Lydia. I think she might have called my name once before, because she says it sort of impatiently. "Nell!"

"What?"

"All right, we've seen what's here. It's not bad. It's really pretty good." She looks over at the rocket ship. "Okay, it's really, really good. But we still can't just disappear."

"I know that," I say. "I've got it figured out."

So we go back to Lydia's rocket ship—that's already how I think of it—and we sit down in the control room while I tell her my plan. I've thought this out carefully. I'm not an idiot—I know that even mothers as unenthusiastic as ours would eventually notice if we disappear every day.

"So how do we do this?" asks Lydia, tipping her chair back as far as it will go.

"We just walk out the door," I say.

She laughs. "That'd be nice."

She stops laughing when I reach into my backpack and hand her a piece of paper.

It reads:

Dear Mrs. McAllister:

We are very pleased to offer your daughter, Lydia, a full scholarship to attend Camp Elegant Earth, the only day camp devoted to designing and creating breathtaking jewelry from recycled products.
We will show our talented campers how to make earrings from erasers, how to turn bicycles chains into necklaces, and how to turn yogurt cartons into bracelets. And don't forget our famous aluminum can pants!

Lydia's school has nominated her as a student who cares deeply about our planet's future. She'll be one of only five campers awarded a free camp registration this year. If you and Lydia are interested in this completely free opportunity to help our planet, we will pick up our campers each morning from several meeting points throughout Birmingham. The closest meeting point to your address is Avondale Library on 40th Street South, where Lydia may catch the Camp Elegant Earth Bus. (Bringing the students in one vehicle is so much better for our environment than hundreds of separate cars!)

Camp begins on May 30 and ends on August 1, with pickup each day at 9 A.M. and drop-off in the same location at 7 P.M. Please have Lydia packed and waiting at the designated pickup spot on May 30.

Sincerely,
Deborah Stalopfield
www.campelegantearth.com

P.S. Dogs are welcome at camp! In fact, they give us much-needed material for our popular dog-hair soccer socks.

"She'll never believe this is a real camp," Lydia says, once she's stopped giggling.

"It is a real camp."

She clearly doesn't believe me.

"Look up the Web site when you get home. I'm telling you, there's a camp for everything. This wasn't even the most ridiculous one."

That would be Camp Flips Not Lips, where a bunch of kids make a pledge not to kiss anyone until they turn eighteen. To take their mind off all that potential kissing, they focus on gymnastics and acrobatics, and they have an hour of trampoline time each day. Even Lydia's mom, who loves camps of all kinds, would be suspicious of that one.

"I still don't think she'll go for it," says Lydia. "I mean, I get to bring Saban with me? That's not very realistic."

"It is so realistic! That letter's even on Camp Elegant Earth stationery," I say. I'm very proud of that stationery—I designed a planet with a ring around it, like Saturn. Only this planet is surrounded by a circle of bracelets and necklaces and pants. "Your mom will look it up on the Internet, and she'll know it's for real. She'll want it to be real. You're underestimating how much she wants you out of the house."

"Good point." Lydia carefully folds up the paper. "Are you sending your mom the same letter?"

"Not exactly."

I pull out another piece of paper:

Dear Mrs. Conway:

We regret to inform you that Nell requires remedial work in social studies. She'll be expected

to attend citywide summer classes at Avondale
Middle School starting on May 30. Classes will
be from 9 A.M. until 7 P.M. each day. Classes
will continue through August 1. Please send a sack
lunch with your child each day.

Please contact me directly at dstalopfield@gmail.
com to let me know if your daughter will be able to
attend these classes. We look forward to meeting
Nell, and we hope this summer will lead her to
make better choices in the future. We regret that
you may be forced to sacrifice your own time with
your daughter for the next two months in order to
help her academic progress.

Sincerely,
Deborah Stalopfield

Assistant to the Assistant Superintendant of Schools,
High–Risk Division

Lydia frowns at me. "You made an A in social studies."

"She never looks at my report card."

"She doesn't know you always make A's?"

"Nope. She does not know that."

"So what happens when she e-mails Deborah Stalopfield?"
asks Lydia.

"I set up a gmail account. I am Deborah Stalopfield. I'll

e-mail her back. Then, five days from now, I'll just walk out of the house on May thirtieth, and we'll start setting up things here."

Lydia looks at her own sheet of paper again. "Huh. And at nine A.M., my mom has to be at work, and she'll have to drop me off early at the library. She won't know that a Camp Elegant Earth bus never comes."

"Or just tell her you'll walk." Avondale Library and Avondale Middle School are both about a mile away. No highways to cross—just neighborhood streets.

Lydia chews her lip for a moment. I can practically hear her brain humming.

"What if my mom calls the camp?" she asks.

"Yeah, that's the main danger," I say. "If she says she's going to, tell her that the principal gave you Deborah Stalopfield's e-mail address and that she travels so much she's almost never reachable by phone."

"What if our moms talk?"

"That's the beauty of your mom hating my mom at the moment. She won't go within twenty feet of her."

Lydia has a few more questions, so we talk a little longer. Then we both get quiet and just spin around in our chairs. I'm pumped on adrenalin, giddy about escaping for two whole months. And I'm realizing I'm not just excited about getting away *from* something—I'm excited about coming *to* something. Coming to this hidden place that's been waiting for us to rediscover it.

Still, underneath the excitement, I'm starting to feel

sleepy. A little nauseous even. It must be one or two o'clock in the morning.

"Let's head back," I say. "We need to find another spot to get over the fence, then we'll need to walk back to where we left the blanket. Mom'll notice if it's not on my bed in the morning."

CHAPTER 6

THE GOING-AWAY PARTY

The next morning, when the "mail" comes, my mother is every bit as thrilled by my remedial classes as I thought she would be. She sits me down at the table and talks sternly to me about trying harder in school, and I nod my head and look depressed.

"You need to think about how *you* are responsible for getting yourself into this situation," she says. "*You* made certain decisions. You've done this all by yourself."

I fight back a grin and keep my head down. She's right—I did this all by myself. And so far it's working out perfectly.

I go to my room for most of the afternoon—Mom thinks it's so I can think about actions and consequences, but it's really so I can start planning a summer at Lodema. It's after five P.M. when I come back into the den, and I'm still trying to hide my good mood.

But Mom seems to have had a mood change herself. She turns toward me and smiles a real smile. She's not wearing any makeup, and her hair is soft with curls falling around her shoulders. I smile back at her without meaning to.

"So I was thinking that you've only got four more days at home," she says. "We should do something special. I made your favorite for supper."

I look toward the kitchen and wonder how I missed it. The air is heavy with the smell of chili. I open my mouth to speak, and I can almost taste the meat and spices on my tongue already. My mom never makes chili in the summer—I usually have to wait until at least November before she'll consider it.

"I just need to put the corn bread in the oven," she says. "And then I thought we could go out to a movie. Your pick."

This is when my mother is most dangerous—when she decides that the idea of being a mom is appealing. When she turns into the mother I've always wanted. It's not as impossible as you might think. This mood falls, obviously, into the herbivore category. She's not showing any sharp teeth at all. But she's like a big-eyed, fluffy, squeezable herbivore. A deer, maybe. When she chooses to be, Mom is sweet and funny. Beautiful and charming, and there's a part of me that really wants to make her happy. To keep her happy. To keep her smiling like this, at me, day after day after day.

"Can we go see *Outrun the Apocalypse*?" I ask. "They're showing it on the big screen in Railroad Park tonight."

My mother hates movies based on video games. She hates sci-fi. And she especially hates movies about the end of the world. So this movie has three strikes against it. I breathe in the chili while I wait for her to answer.

She shrugs. "Sure. If you want. It's going to be one of those where all the women wear tight leather pants and carry guns, isn't it?"

"Probably," I say.

"I don't want to sit on the ground," she says. "But I'm up for it as long as we can find the folding chairs."

She stands and walks past me, running her hand through my hair. I watch her pour oil in the cast-iron skillet and turn on the oven. She looks toward me, and her brown eyes are wide and deep. She's really extremely pretty. Sometimes I wish I had her eyes.

"Lionel should be home any second," she says. "Would you rather it just be us at the movies, or would you like to invite him?"

"I'd like him to come," I say. "And I'll set the table."

I'm glad Lionel's coming home. He makes conversation easier—he chats about nothing and everything, and even if Mom and I start making little jabs at each other, he keeps on talking like we're just trading compliments. He's sort of a protective cushion between us. If we have awkward silences, he fills them up.

I like setting the table for three better than setting it for two. It feels more substantial. I grab a handful of silverware and three plates. Mom used to make fun of me when I was younger for always pestering her to let me set the table. She said kids were supposed to hate setting the table because it's a chore. "Chore" means you shouldn't like doing it. And she's always preferred to eat in front of the television with her plate in her lap. But sitting down for a real meal at the table has always made me feel like I'm on a television show, like we're all acting out parts and saying our lines, and that when we clear our plates and head back to the rest of our lives, we might keep reading our scripts. I think life would surely go better if we had scripts.

I still feel like that, even though I'm too old for pretend. But I straighten the knives and line up the spoons next to them, and part of me thinks when we get up from this table, maybe we'll be a different family.

The front door opens, and Lionel calls out, "Something smells great!"

I wave at him, a napkin in my hand. His shaggy black hair is getting white over his ears, and he'd be handsome except that all his features—nose, mouth, eyebrows, chin—all seem to be a little too big for his face. But his smile is overly big, too, and it's completely handsome.

He gives me a one-armed hug—my head doesn't even reach his shoulder—and then he walks to the stove and gives Mom the same hug, plus a quick kiss on her cheek. He used to give her two-armed hugs with real kisses on the mouth. Those made me groan and turn my head—who wants to watch kisses on the mouth, especially when the kissee is your mother? But I wish they'd start doing it again now. Over the years, I've learned that the shift from two-armed hugs to one-armed hugs is a sign that a stepfather might be on his way out.

"What did you do to get chili in May?" Lionel asks me, walking back into the den and stooping to pick up the newspaper. "What are we celebrating?"

"Remedial social studies classes," I say happily. "All summer long."

"Oh," he says. "Well, that wasn't my first guess. I thought

you loved social studies. It's been an easy class for you, hasn't it?"

I sneak a glance at Mom, who doesn't seem to have heard. Once upon a time, it used to hurt my feelings that Mom didn't care about my grades. I'd show her a report card with straight A's and she'd blink at it once or twice and hand it back to me without a word. She looked more impressed at a menu for Chinese takeout. Eventually I stopped showing her my grades. I don't show them to Lionel, either, but he asks about tests and stuff. And apparently he pays attention to my answers. Normally that would make me feel all warm and fuzzy—he really is a sweet guy—but right now I'm wishing he paid less attention.

"Yeah, well, ah, the class was harder than I thought, I guess," I say.

"Hmm," he says. "I never thought you'd be taking remedial classes in anything."

"Just because she's good at crosswords doesn't mean she's good at things that matter," calls my mother.

Lionel and I look at each other for a second. I think we're both trying to figure out if she meant to insult one of us or both of us.

"I don't think I said thanks for cooking the chili, Mom," I say, because I want to pretend she didn't mean to insult either one of us. "That was really nice of you."

She nods. Of course, when she's being sweet to me, there's always the part of me waiting for it. Waiting for her to get tired of playing Mom. Waiting for her to get tired of liking me. Waiting for the bad thing to happen. But the minutes or the hours pass and that part of me gets lazy and forgets to be on guard. And then it hurts worse when everything goes bad.

Even though I know the bad thing will happen—that it always happens—I just want, so badly, for it not to happen right now.

"Sure, sweetie," she says. "And, Lionel, those social studies classes mean Nell will be gone most days this summer. It's a full two months."

Lionel's folding the crossword puzzle into a convenient size. When he glances up—and I admit that I feel more flattered than guilty about this—he looks disappointed. Like he'll miss me. It occurs to me that maybe I'm not the only one who likes having a protective cushion around when it comes to Mom.

Lionel doesn't say anything, though. He knows she doesn't want him to question me going away. Lionel is a good guy, but he is an object at rest. He likes to stay at rest. He likes as little conflict as possible.

He rattles the newspaper. "Okay, Nell," he says. "Eight-letter word for 'how we communicate.'"

I count it out on my fingers. "Talking" is a letter short.

"Language," I say after a second.

Dinner goes pretty well, and then we all pack into Lionel's gray Buick. I sit behind Mom because Lionel has to have the driver's seat back as far as it will go. We're only about ten minutes from Railroad Park—it's in the middle of downtown, built along the old railroad tracks. According to Memama and Grandpops, those railroad tracks used to carry people from place to place. Now the trains still run, but they carry materials from place to place . . . sort of like semitrucks, only bigger and louder.

The park is great because you can watch the trains rumble by and hear their whistles blow. You look out over the acres and acres of park, with its flowers and thick grass and waterfalls, and at night the waterfalls are lit up pink and purple and blue with colored spotlights. The skyscrapers of downtown are right over your head—the red lights of City Federal, which look so far away from our golf course, seem like they're just a few feet away when you're lying on the grass in the park.

Every Thursday night, the city shows a different movie on a big inflatable screen set up in the park, and everyone arranges their blankets and chairs on a soft, sloping hill. Children run around and fall down like clumsy puppies. A few feet away from me, there's a little black girl with amazing hair—hundreds of tiny braids—picking clovers with her mother. There's a little white boy trying to stand on his head. All around us, adults are falling asleep. (Lionel is snoring so loud in his chair that I have to poke him in the side a few times.) And some people, like me, are actually watching the movie.

We're about halfway through *Outrun the Apocalypse* when two toddlers, just off to my left, run full speed into a Labrador retriever. They hit its side so hard that their feet leave the ground and they flip over the dog and land on their backs. The dog wags its tail, then there's a whole lot of screaming.

I wait for a second, but I don't see any parents around. So I stand up to go see if I can at least get the dog to quit slobbering all over the kids' faces. It's acting like they're screaming lollipops. Still, it wasn't the dog's fault that the kids were out of control, so I call him a good boy as I push him away with my elbow. The little boys' faces are screwed up so tight that they have no eyes at all, just giant open mouths.

"Hey," I say, touching one of them lightly on the head. "Hey, are you okay? Do you know where your parents are?"

"I'll take him," says a voice. "He's my little brother."

I look up and there's Adam Cooper. The one who can do one-armed push-ups. The one who has never spoken to me. And now he *has* spoken to me, although, of course, he didn't know he was speaking to me. So I need to speak to him. Right.

"Okay," I say. I try to smile.

He scoops the redheaded boy into his arms. The other boy gets to his feet and scrambles off, hopefully to find someone related to him. Adam's brother is still crying, and Adam starts bouncing him up and down a little. He looks from me to his little brother and then back to me again.

"It's Nell, right? Don't you go to my school?" He has to raise his voice so I can hear him over the crying.

"Yeah," I say, and I'm proud of how steady my voice sounds. "Yeah" was a very reasonable response. Not stupid at all. Good call.

"I'm Adam."

"Right," I say. "Your brother, um, ran into a dog."

Hmmm, I think. That response was not quite as good.

"He's a moron," he says, but he says it fondly. Like he *likes* morons. "You here with your parents?"

The little redhead is calming down slightly. He's whimpering instead of screaming.

I nod. "My mom and stepdad. They're both asleep."

It occurs to me suddenly that maybe it'd be better if I were here with Lydia. Or a massive group of friends. Not that I have a massive group of friends.

"You're lucky," he says. "My parents are awake. They think this is good family time."

Okay, good. I feel better about being with Mom and Lionel. "I guess it is if you don't count that your brother's going around attacking Labrador retrievers," I say.

He laughs. "Yeah, he's vicious."

I need to come up with something else to make him laugh. Am I supposed to be thinking this much before every sentence? Can he see the wheels turning in my brain? Still, I would really like to make him laugh again. I look at his brother, who is now quiet and squirming.

"My friend Lydia has a Maltipoo that might be a better match for your brother," I say. "We could put them in a ring and let them fight it out."

"A Maltipoo?"

"Maltese poodle. Very macho."

He does laugh again, and I definitely feel like I am on a television show now. I am playing a character who makes Adam Cooper laugh.

And then I hear my mother's voice.

"Nell, come on back and stop flirting," she says, loudly enough that an old couple in lawn chairs several feet away turn toward us.

I look away from Adam because I can't stand to see his reaction. My mother is a couple of steps away from me. The wind blows her strapless dress around her knees.

"I'm just talking, Mom," I say it in a robot voice, no emotion.

"If you wanted to come here tonight for a date, you should have said so," she says. She flips her hair over her shoulder.

"It's not a date," I say.

Sometimes I think my mother doesn't know me at all, but at other times, like now, I realize she can read every thought in my head. She can tell I like Adam. And she can tell this is, of course, not a date. And she can tell that the thing I want most in the entire world at this moment is for him *not to know that I like him*.

"We just go the same school, ma'am," says Adam. "I hardly know her."

I hear those words, and I try very hard to keep my face blank so my mother doesn't see into my head. But I feel like I just ran full speed into a Labrador retriever and hit the ground hard.

"You can come sit with us," Mom says to Adam, "if you'd like."

"No, that's okay," he says, and I hear how much he wants to escape. I know the sound of wanting to escape.

"Well," he says to me, "see you."

"Bye," I say. My feet step on my mother's shadow as we walk back to our chairs.

"He's a nice-looking boy," my mother says cheerfully. "He's got good bones. I bet he's got plenty of girls after him."

What I hear her say is that he would never pick me, not

when he has so many better options. Prettier, smarter, more likable options. I might also be hearing her say that she's doing me a favor by keeping me from getting my hopes up.

"If you were trying to embarrass me, it worked," I say.

She laughs. No, it's more of a giggle.

"Don't be ridiculous," she says. "No one's trying to embarrass you."

I wonder if she believes that. I wonder if I believe it. Part of me thinks *of course* your mother wouldn't want to embarrass you. Why would she? What would she get out of it? And I don't have an answer to that.

But another part of me knows without a doubt that she did mean to embarrass me. I don't know why she does it, but I know that she does. And as I steal looks at her in her pink sundress, long legs crossed so gracefully, I know that she thinks if she were my age, she would be one of those prettier, smarter, more likable girls that Adam would be interested in. I think she's probably right.

A few years ago, before I had really developed my strategy, I would try to get back at Mom when she acted like this. When I was furious and hurt, I'd find ways to get revenge without her knowing. I sprayed Windex on her toothbrush. I let Saban lick her favorite coffee mug and then I put it back in the cabinet. I'd eat all the pecans in the mixed nuts because they're her favorite.

That was kid's stuff. I've learned that revenge doesn't help you feel better. It makes you feel guilty, when what you really need is not to feel anything. Feelings are the whole problem. Anger, hurt, sadness, guilt—it's all too much. The only thing that really helps is to stop feeling altogether.

To stop feeling, you have to disappear. So that's what I do. For the rest of the night, I think of my body as a robot that stands up and walks to the car and then walks to my bedroom and brushes my teeth and gets in bed, while that whole time the real me is gone. The real me is wandering around Lodema and setting up a new home inside a dinosaur. The robot deals with my mother, nods at her when necessary, while the real me walks barefoot on cool fake grass and looks up at the moon.

The next morning, I head to see my grandparents. I feel like I'm back inside my body. I will not think about Adam Cooper anymore. I have more important things to think about, and my grandparents can help me.

I hug and kiss them both, breathe in Grandpops's grassy smell, and then I plop down on the sofa. I take a long moment to look at them both, from Memama's small, perfect hands to Grandpops's stubbly cheeks. I can't stand to lie to them about remedial classes—I assume eventually Mom will tell them.

I see Memama flash a look at Grandpops, a look that is like a kiss.

I think of Adam Cooper's face while he was laughing, and then I think of him saying, "I hardly know her."

I need to focus. I need to concentrate on planning for Lodema. That's what matters.

"Memama, I need a favor," I say. "I need you to teach me how to cook a fish."

CHAPTER 7
THE NEW WORLD

Finally it's May 30. I hug Mom and Lionel good-bye at about 8:30 and tell them I'm going to walk to the middle school. Mom tries to neaten my hair, and Lionel hugs me extra hard. I walk out the front door and around the block before looping back to the golf course.

I'm only carrying my backpack—I figure I can take a few things each day, and today I've focused on the basics to make Marvin feel like home. Lydia and I have plenty of time to think through our supply list—the bigger issue has been figuring out how to get in and out of Lodema in the daylight without anyone noticing. Vaulting over grass like knives everyday isn't going to work. I've spent the last few days walking the perimeter of the golf course, looking for the best place for Lydia and me to climb the fence. We'll want to stay off the streets and sidewalks as much as possible.

I've found a spot with a crape myrtle growing close to the outside of the fence, and the tree is surrounded by high shrubs. We can climb the tree instead of the fence, and the shrubs will hide us. Plus there's nothing but weeds on the other side—no sharp pampas grass. It's perfect, and as I make my way there with my backpack, wading through the weeds, I only have one small worry: painted on the side of the crape myrtle are the same symbols we saw on the side of the empty aquarium. Green arrow, purple circles, blue eyebrows. Lydia and I have hardly talked over the last few days—we figured we should do everything possible to keep her mom from getting suspicious—so I haven't told her about it yet. She might have something smart to say. Or she might just talk more about tadpoles and snow.

I decide to walk to the Chevron. I have a sandwich and an apple in my lunch bag, but I'd like to buy a little treat for our first day on the course. Plus I always like any excuse to go to a gas station. I like the smell of gas, I like the snack marts, and I like all those people driving off to faraway places. Or even just across town. If you want to get somewhere, if you want to put some distance between yourself and where you started, you have to get friendly with gas stations.

I look both ways before I cross the street, not just looking for traffic, but looking for anyone who might know me. I jog across Clairmont Avenue quickly, keeping one hand up to shield my face. The gas station is just ahead of me on the corner.

The truth is that our options are going to be very limited by not having a car. This isn't New York or Boston—Birmingham is not a walking city. Everyone has cars here, and even though you could ride the bus, it's really inconvenient. (We had a neighbor who worked in a restaurant five miles away, and it took her two stops and over an hour to get to work every morning.) A few people ride bicycles, but there aren't any bike paths; if you ride on major roads, you have a death wish. So that leaves walking. At least that's what's left for me and Lydia. And that means we're within a half hour of a couple of nice restaurants, a used bookstore, a gourmet grocery store, and the Chevron.

My entire savings adds up to thirty dollars. That gourmet grocery store is definitely off-limits.

At the gas station, I linger over the food aisles, trying to memorize what's on the shelves. If we need extra supplies, this is where we'll have to come. (Man, beef jerky is expensive. You'd think it was dried diamonds, not dried cow.) I head to the counter with a Snickers—my favorite candy bar— and a Heath bar, Lydia's favorite.

The girl at the counter is by far the most beautiful person I've ever seen working in a gas station. She has a short afro and creamy brown skin, and she's slouching over the counter in a way that makes her seem confident and cool. It's the kind of slouch that I could see myself practicing. I wonder if Adam Cooper likes slouchers.

Nope. I will not think of him. When I think of him, I see my mother's face.

"I like your shirt," says the pretty sloucher, handing me my change.

"Thanks," I say. "My dad got it for me from Spain."

That's true. It has a mosaic bull on it. I can't remember why Dad went to Spain, but I think it may have been a trip with a girlfriend.

"You've been to Spain?" she asks.

"I haven't been anywhere."

She gives me a sympathetic, I-get-you look. I like her a lot better than the hairy guy with a mustache who's usually at the counter. He has a tattoo of what I think is a koala on his neck.

I head back to the honeysuckle tree to wait for Lydia. When she shows up a little while later, she's sweating and out of breath. She's got Saban's leash in one hand: his tongue is hanging out of his mouth, and he's sort of staggering.

I pull out a bottle of water from my backpack.

"Thanks," she says. She takes a long chug, then she unzips her bag and pulls out Saban's water dish. She pours him half of the water.

"Did you have any trouble?" I ask.

"Nope. Mom made me pancakes for breakfast, squeezed me hard for a second, and then said she was running late for work. I think she's looking forward to me bringing back a pair of those aluminum can pants."

As soon as Lydia's rested, we pick up our backpacks and climb the crape myrtle, with Lydia passing Saban over the fence to me once I get on the golf-course side. We head to the putt-putt course. The second I open the door to Marvin, I realize we have a problem. The heat knocks the breath out of me. I haven't been in Marvin during the heat of the day—he's like a sauna. In the amount of time it takes to walk in, set down my bag and unzip it, my hair is drenched like I just got out of the shower. I go back outside and Lydia's standing in the shade of her rocket ship. Neither one of us can quite make ourselves go inside again.

"I think I can be done setting up in maybe thirty minutes," I say. "Meet you back here then. We can go find a nice shady tree or something."

"You know, you could take the other bunk bed in my rocket," Lydia says. "There's plenty of room for us both."

"No, thanks," I say. "I want my own place. Or, you know, my own dinosaur."

She shrugs, takes a breath, and darts inside the rocket ship. Plenty of kids at school hate being by themselves—they're never without a group of friends around them laughing and talking. The worst punishment for them is if a teacher makes them sit alone at lunch. I've never been forced to sit by myself at lunch, but it wouldn't be so bad, really. It'd be the perfect time to read a book. (The same thing occurs to me about being sent to prison—just having to sit on a bunk bed all day long might be kind of nice. You could read and draw and learn how to do things like paint or play the guitar. I think I could be okay with prison.)

Anyway, Lydia and I both like to have time to ourselves. Neither of us has brothers or sisters, and I think that has something to do with it. There are plenty of times that I have to entertain myself—there's no one else around to do it. If I hated alone time, my life would be pretty miserable. Instead I've learned to enjoy it, and I miss it if I don't have it.

Despite all these positive thoughts about alone time, even a minute inside Marvin is miserable. I think I might pass out. But I prop the door open, so there's a little breeze. I start to think I can handle it. I pull out an inflatable mattress, the kind you float on in the swimming pool. I blow it up—outside in the shade of an oak tree—and bring it back into Marvin. It's a pretty good couch. I pull out my Lava lamp and plug it in, just to see if the electricity works. It does. Between the inflated mattress and the floating blue shadows on the wall from the Lava lamp, I'm really feeling an underwater theme in here. It's more like being in the belly of a whale than a dinosaur.

I pull out my laptop, which is wrapped in a blanket. It's time to leave Marvin. I need to get closer to some of the houses lining the golf course.

Once I went to the beach down at Gulf Shores, and I met a boy from Philadelphia. We caught mussels together for a while, snatching them up in the surf and then tossing them back so they could bury themselves in the wet sand again. It was his first time to Alabama, and he said that before he came down here he thought nobody owned any shoes. And nobody had electricity. That made me think: 1) he had been watching some very old movies; 2) he was sort of condescending for someone who lived in a city known for cream cheese; and 3) my state has an unfair reputation.

I know some people think we're still all about dirt roads and hound dogs down here. But I've lived in a big city all my life. I don't want Lodema to be some big camping trip. I don't want to just fish and wander around dirty and barefooted. I need the Internet. And I don't want to have to walk all the way back to my house to get it.

I should mention that I did one other thing during the last four days. I started hanging out along 34th Street, the street that's closest to the putt-putt course. The backyards of those houses are only forty or fifty feet from the fence around Lodema. I took my scooter to 34th Street and rode up and down the sidewalk during the afternoons when people were getting home from work. I struck up conversations with people and complimented them on their pets. I asked the people's names. Then I asked for their pets' names, and I scratched plenty of dogs behind their ears while I oohed and aahed over them. I found out what kinds of dogs they were. I found out from the pet owners if any of their neighbors had pets. I bet I know the names of at least twenty dogs and cats that live on 34th Street.

When I boot up my laptop and call up the list of available networks, I recognize several of the networks that are labeled by last names. Anderson. Bailey. Watson. Levey. Sanchez. All of them are security-enabled networks requiring a password. This is where it gets fun. I know how people love to use their pets' names for passwords. Birthdays and anniversaries, too, but those are a lot harder to figure out. So I play around with different combinations—pumpkin, pumpkintheboxer, lady, ladycollie, sam, schnauzer, samschnauzer, samtheschnauzer, labradoodle, dixie, dixielab, dixielabradoodle—and pretty soon I have it: the Watsons' password is eugenebeagle. I'm in.

Soon I've got a wireless connection whenever I want it, and both our places are hot but comfortable. I see that Lydia's even brought a little fan, which she's angled right over her bed. Saban lies in front of it with his tongue hanging out. He raises his head occasionally, then looks disappointed and flops back down.

"Should we walk him?" I ask. "He seems depressed."

"He always looks like that."

"Huh."

Regardless of Saban's opinion, we're ready to get out in the fresh air. We grab our lunches and a couple of bottles of water. We don't bother putting Saban on a leash. It's not like he can go very far. But we haven't even left the putt-putt course before Lydia's yanking on my arm.

"What?"

"Look," Lydia says, pointing toward the aquarium hole.

I do look, but all I see is the concrete and the fake grass and those three fish mouths. *"What?"*

She strides over and leans down by the three fish. Saban pants along beside her. When she stands up, she's holding something in her hand. I look closer. It's a Coke can.

"This wasn't here last week," she says. "Someone else has been here."

I think about that. It hadn't occurred to me that anyone else would come on the course, but it doesn't seem like a huge deal.

"Maybe it's kids," I say. "Serial litterers. Or maybe there's still a maintenance guy who checks on things."

"And that doesn't worry you?"

"Not really," I say. "I think there's a good chance the wind just blew that can over here. It's one Coke can. And this place is huge. What are the chances of running into anybody *if* someone's here?"

"If somebody's on this golf course, it'd be nice to know who," says Lydia. "I might walk into my rocket one day and find some guy waving a knife."

Have I mentioned that there's a downside to Lydia watching all those horror movies?

"You mean some guy waving a Coke," I say.

"I just think it's strange," Lydia says. "That's all. This place is supposed to be abandoned. But if there is a guy with a knife, I've been practicing this kickboxing move that might be perfect."

She demonstrates, lifting one leg off the ground and bringing her hands up in a boxing position. She twists and leans back a little, then bends her knee and rams the heel of her foot into my shoulder.

"Ow!"

"Right?" she says, pleased. "And if you had a knife, don't you think you would have dropped it?"

She's lucky that I think being weird is a good thing.

Rubbing my shoulder, I start walking and tell her to come on. I don't plan to waste anymore energy thinking about the Coke can or imaginary knives. We have a new world to discover.

We set a pretty fast pace and keep within sight of the fence, hoping to make a complete loop around the course before it gets dark. I'll admit, we get a little sidetracked. Even with the constant itchy weeds and swarms of gnats and mosquitoes, the golf course is fascinating. We see the flag for Hole Four at the top of a wide, steep hill. The top of the hill is flat like a crater, and the white sand of the sand traps catches the sunlight. We plow through the grass and hike up the hill. When we get to the top, panting, it's obvious we're on what used to be the green. The grass is thicker and nicer than most of the course—no weeds, just tall, soft green blades. It makes me wish all grass was like the grass on the putt-putt course, that it didn't grow at all. Then we'd be standing on a carpet-grassed green like on television, and we could lie down and take a nap on it.

Needing a break, we sit down even though the spot isn't quite as nice as carpet. We flatten out a patch by making grass angels, then we lie back and catch our breaths. That's when we notice that you have a perfect view of the airplanes landing and taking off at the airport, which is maybe ten miles away. When we're flat on our backs, we can see the white underbellies of the planes as they go over us. The Southwest planes look like orange and purple birds gliding through the sky, and when they get close you see their red bellies. They're by far the most colorful ones. It's like we've found some hidden island where giant, prehistoric birds still live, and we can observe them secretly. I smile at that idea: This white bird-plane is going off to find food for its nest. The next bird-plane is coming home to rest for the night. That last one is going so high and so straight that it just enjoys the feel of flying.

We shake the grass out of our hair and walk until we come to Hole Six, which is another steep climb. We're curious if we can see the planes better from here, but instead we're looking into downtown Birmingham. Just below us, we see the Western Supermarket and the stoplight on 22nd Street. Then lots of flat gray roofs. But past that, the view of the city is breathtaking. I look away from the lights and peer downhill—there's something about steep hills that makes me want to roll down them. So I do. I lie down and push off, and soon I'm tumbling so fast that everything is a green and blue blur. I keep picking up speed—if I were a boulder on a mountain, I'd be starting an avalanche. If I were an airplane on a runway, I'd be lifting into the air. I shriek and I taste grass in my mouth. Then I'm at the bottom, breathless, my head spinning. It's like the end of a roller coaster: First of all, I'm possibly ready to throw up. Second of all, I'm thinking I need to do it all over again.

As I'm sitting up, I hear a thumping sound and a squeal. Lydia is coming down the hill, too. She lands a few feet from me.

"That was amazing!" she says, still lying sprawled across the ground, her eyes squeezed shut. "Let's do it again!"

So we do. And before we know it, the sky has turned orange and pink, and we have to start jogging home. We don't want to make our moms suspicious on our first day.

As we head away from Hole Six, we see movement off to our left, close to one of the ponds we haven't explored. At first I think it's just a tree in the wind, but then I see a shadow. Not a tree shadow. A person shadow.

"Lydia," I whisper.

She stops and turns back to me. "What?"

"Over there."

"I don't see anything."

She starts walking, but I'm slower to move. I decide Lydia's talk about some Coke-drinking boogeyman has made me paranoid. We pick up the pace and barely make it back into our own yards before the sun completely sets.

CHAPTER 8
THE CHEWY CENTER

As we climb over the crape myrtle and drop down to the golf course on our second day at Lodema, we make a plan. So far we've stayed close to the edges of the golf course. If Lodema were a piece of Valentine's candy, then we've only nibbled around the chewy center. It could be caramel or coconut or that disgusting orange crème—we don't know. So that's the goal for the day—check out the chewy center and find out what's in there.

First we need to visit the putt-putt course and drop off our second batch of supplies. Today I filled my backpack mostly with snacks. Next to my inflatable float/couch, I stack up the food I've brought—peanut butter, bread, crackers, dried apples. A big can of peanuts and a box of raisins. I had to limit my food supplies to things that didn't need to be refrigerated and that Mom wouldn't miss from the pantry.

I fill one corner with a few other supplies: mosquito spray, roach spray, Band-Aids, soap. A plastic bowl, an iron skillet, a plate, and a fork. A bathing suit and a change of clothes, just in case.

Lydia sticks her head inside Marvin as I'm folding my extra T-shirt.

"An underground city built by monkeys," she says.

"A pirate ship with chests full of gold," I answer.

We've been doing this all morning—seeing who can come up with the strangest, most impossible things we might find today. Of course, it's more likely that we'll find nothing but weeds and maybe another pond or two. Or snakes. I'm still watching for snakes.

"How could a ship get on a golf course?" asks Lydia.

"I don't know," I say, "but that's why it'd be such a great hiding place. No one would think to look."

We head straight toward the center of Lodema. We head past Marvin and the putt-putt course, and if we look over our shoulders we see a dinosaur and a rocket ship and a volcano behind us, and, past that, the city skyline. After ten or fifteen minutes of walking, we can't see much of anything but the tall grass up past our waists and pine trees all around us. We stumble across a concrete path—an old golf cart path, I guess—and after that the walking gets easier.

"It doesn't look like the monkeys are going to happen," I say, wiping the sweat off my forehead. My hair is sticking to me, pieces of grass are sticking to me, and I think some gnats might be sticking to me.

"Maybe an enchanted castle where everyone inside has been asleep for a hundred years," says Lydia. "Like Sleeping Beauty."

"Or maybe . . ."

"Don't even start about the snakes again," she says.

We plod on, taking swigs of water as we go. When we first see the castle, I think Lydia was right about Sleeping Beauty. We come around a bend in the path and instead of just tree-tops and sky, we see the top of a stone building. It's falling apart, with big gaps and holes in the roof and walls, but on one side there's definitely a turret like in fairy tales.

"If there's a princess in there, I'm not kissing her," I say.

"Come on!" says Lydia, and she starts running through the grass. I'm so close behind her that the grass she stomps down slaps back against my thighs. It's dry and scratchy against my skin, but it makes a whispering sound as we run like it has a secret to tell us.

Once we get closer to the stone building, we can tell there's not a sleeping princess inside. For one thing, it's too small to be a real castle. It's barely bigger than the kitchen of our apartment. But mainly what rules out the princess idea is a faded blue and white sign that says CONCESSIONS hanging over a boarded up window. I suppose it's blocking the open space where people used to sell drinks and snacks. I've heard that before Lodema was a golf course, it was a big park with a merry-go-round and paddleboats and maybe a Ferris wheel. I never really believed it, but the concession stand makes me wonder. I've never heard of a concession stand on a golf course.

The bottom of the concession castle seems pretty solid, but the farther up it goes, the more stones are missing. Sky and trees show through the holes. Kudzu has crept into the cracks, and pink buttercups are growing along the walls. Even though we know it's just a place where people bought Cokes and popcorn, it still feels like some forgotten enchanted hiding place. Maybe not a place where kings and queens lived, but a place where you might find a talking bear or a family of gnomes.

"Can we get in?" I ask.

Lydia shrugs and starts around the left side of the building. "Don't know," she says. "I'll go this way, and you look on the other side."

I check around the left side, and I only see a small window too tall for me to reach. If there was ever glass in it, it's long gone now. I hear Lydia's voice calling me, and when I reach her, she's holding a weathered piece of plywood propped against the wall. She grins and slides the wood back, and I can see that there's a hole behind it. A hole wider than my shoulders and nearly as high as my waist.

"This sort of counts as a door," says Lydia.

There's something about squeezing through a small space that makes whatever's on the other side seem more exciting somehow. Like how if you walk through an open gate into someone's yard, it's just a normal yard. But if you squeeze through a little hole in a fence, turning and twisting and trying not to cut yourself or rip your clothes, by the time you pop out the other side, you just *expect* to find something worth all that effort.

At first, though, as I stand up inside the stone walls, it seems like I might be disappointed. There's a concrete floor and empty shelves on the walls. Grass is growing through the cracks in the concrete. And there's a narrow wooden staircase that leads up to what was maybe a storage space. Now the storage space opens up to the sky. The roof of the building is totally gone.

Sunlight and shadows dance across the ground as I look up at the staircase. I look back at Lydia, who's brushing a spiderweb out of her hair.

"Let's go," she says.

We're careful as we go up the stairs. They creak and groan under our feet. Some of the railing is missing, and the wood is cracking like the old paint in our apartment. I wonder when the last pair of feet stepped on these stairs. But we get to the top stair without any catastrophes. Not only is the roof gone, but the walls are only a couple of feet high, with plenty of stones missing. The whole place is damp and dirty and sprinkled with bird poop.

Then we look over the edge of the walls, and it's suddenly worth climbing the stairs. We're looking onto a fat, smallish tree. It's got pointy wide leaves, so maybe it's a maple. And in the tree I can see at least a dozen birds' nests. Some have white eggs, some have brown eggs, and some have blue speckled eggs. Some have grown-up birds perched in them, and a few of them look up and squawk at us. In one small nest near the top of the tree, I can see two baby birds, almost translucent, hardly any feathers at all. They stretch open their beaks and scream to be fed. The eggs, though, are peaceful and quiet. It's like we've found a bird day-care center.

"It's a whole city of nests," I say.

"Maybe we can get a baby," says Lydia.

"No way," I say. "Not unless we have to. We are not doing that again."

We found a baby bird in Lydia's backyard once, and Marvin—the stepdad, not the dinosaur—told us to feed him milk with a medicine dropper. We made a little nest in a shoebox and tried to feed him twice a day. He never seemed to care for the milk much, so we dug for worms and grubs and tried those. But he just got weaker. Eventually he died and we had to bury him out by the honeysuckle tree. Mom told me that we should never have picked him up because his mother probably would have found him. She said you should never touch a baby bird because if you make the baby smell like a human, his mother won't want him anymore. I think that's lousy parenting. But I guess even a hard-to-please mother bird would have done a better job of raising that baby bird than we did. I still feel guilty when I remember how light it was in that shoebox, no more weight than the bow off a birthday present. How pale its skin was and how its heart pounded in its rib cage. He was ours to take care of, and we let him down.

I don't want another baby bird. They weigh too heavy on me.

It's only as we're leaving that I notice the wall right at the edge of the staircase. I had my back turned to it as we were coming up to the turret. But I suddenly realize that maybe another pair of feet have walked up these stairs more recently than I thought. I see the same signs we saw in the aquarium and on the crape myrtle. Only this time it's not painted—it's a chalk drawing. A pale green arrow, lavender circles, and sky-blue dashes. We stop and stare at it, and Lydia runs her finger over the arrow. The tip of her finger comes away green.

"Nell, wouldn't chalk wash off when it rains?" asks Lydia.

"Yeah," I say. "I think."

"And it rained last Friday, right? So somebody drew this since then?"

"Or maybe it's a special kind of chalk," I say, not believing it, but not wanting Lydia to start kickboxing again. "A kind that lasts for years."

"Right," she says. "Sure."

I do not want anyone else to be here. I want this to be our own private kingdom. So I block out the Coke can and the chalk signs and refuse to think about them anymore. My mind is very good at blocking out unpleasant things.

When I get home that afternoon, Mom is sitting on the back patio—a little concrete square, but "patio" sounds better—in her light blue lounge chair. She's got one knee bent, and she's hunched over her toes with a bottle of nail polish in one hand.

"Bring out the other chair," she says. "I'll do yours, too."

Lying in the sun is one of the things my mother really likes to do. Painting her nails while the sun beats down on her is maybe her favorite thing in the world. I don't particularly like to sit in the sun—it's too hot—and I don't really care about doing my nails.

"That sounds fun," I say, and go to pull the other chair from under the stairway.

If I didn't say that—if I said something like, "I don't really feel like it"—she'd say, "Okay." But the way she'd say it, clipped and pinched, would make it obvious that it's not okay. That I've hurt her feelings. Mom can be very sensitive when it comes to getting her feelings hurt. Lionel uses that word about her a lot, and he says it in a sort of complimentary way, like artists are sensitive and geniuses are sensitive.

"Left foot first," Mom says, when I have my chair arranged. I stick my ankle toward her, and she props my foot on her knee.

"Relax," she says. "Lie down."

There's a part of me that would like to tell her about my day. I'd like to try to explain how the sky looked like a blue ceiling over the stone walls and how some of the birds' nests had little bits of colored cloth and string—red, yellow, and even a flash of purple—woven into them. I'd like to tell her what it's like to roll down a hill so fast that I can't feel my arms and legs anymore. I have these impulses occasionally—the need to talk and talk until she finally understands me. The need to describe what's inside my head and hope that if I get the words right, she'll finally know me and like me and really *see* me. I don't say anything, though. Partly that's because I know if I confess about the golf course, I'll probably never get to set foot there again.

But the bigger reason is that if half of me wants to tell Mom about what I've found, the other half of me wants to never mention a word about anything I've seen in the last week. That part of me feels like I should put every single sight and sound and memory into a box, dig a hole, and make sure no one can ever touch any of it. Because it's mine.

I hand over a lot of things when I'm home. Mom tells me she doesn't like a shirt I want to buy, and I hand it over. Not the shirt itself, but my wish for that shirt. I want to watch one television show and she wants to watch another one—I hand that over, too. It's easier that way. I even hand over my toenails when she asks. But I think sometimes you need to put a thing in a box—even if the box is inside your head—and store it away for yourself.

When our toenails are done, Mom lies down, and it's quiet for a while. She hums under her breath a little.

"Did you have a good day?" she asks.

"Pretty good," I say.

"It's not too bad there?"

"No," I say. "It's not bad."

"I'm impressed that you haven't complained once," she says. "I'd have been a lot grumpier about summer school."

This is why it's worth acting happy about getting my toenails painted. Mom likes me when we're lying like this, side by side, shiny-skinned. She's smiling underneath her sweat mustache. I feel my shoulders relax, and I start to enjoy the stretchy feel of the chair underneath me. When she speaks, she turns her head to me without opening her eyes.

"Sometimes I think we could just pack up the car and leave one day," she says. "Just leave the furniture behind us, fill up the car with gas, and drive until we hit the ocean. Or the mountains. I could get a job waiting tables—because there's always a restaurant needing waitresses—and when I wasn't working, I'd lie on the beach. And I'd have a garden."

Have I mentioned that my mom talks about escaping, too? She likes to think about how she could just walk away from her life and start a whole new one. Sometimes those conversations are sad and a little scary—does she really hate her life here so much?—but sometimes they're sort of fun.

"We could get a dog," she says. "You could pick him out."

I smile. "A big one or a little one?"

"Whatever you wanted. As long as he doesn't dig up my garden."

I think about Saban running along the beach, and I think he'd be afraid of the waves. "I think I'll get an Irish setter," I say.

"Good choice," she says. "I like Irish setters."

When we're lying like this, she thinks we're the same.

"You can have space in the garden, too," she says. "You can grow all the strawberries you want."

"I'd like to grow corn," I say. I have a picture in my mind of a corn maze, which I've read about. I'd like to be able to get lost in my rows of corn.

"Okay," she says. "You might need to get a job, too, of course, when you're old enough. You could wait tables and they'd give you great tips because you're young and pretty."

When her eyes are closed, she thinks I'm pretty. I am warm and sleepy and I think how I like the sound of her voice.

CHAPTER 9
A HANDFUL OF CHALK

For the next week or so, Lydia and I have a set routine. We drop off any odds and ends at the putt-putt course, and we hang out around Marvin or the rocket ship until about eleven o'clock, when the heat gets so bad we can't stand it. We check the nests and see if anyone else has hatched. We eat our lunch somewhere shady, then we explore some more. The day we found the blackberry patch, we ate until our fingers were dyed purple. The day we found the two box turtles, we spent an hour trying to make them race. (Turtles are apparently not competitive animals.) Sometimes it's a slow day and we wind up just playing cards or climbing trees, but, no matter what, in late afternoon we head over to Hole Four to watch the airplanes.

We're into our second week of Lodema before we discover the clover field. We've just finished checking on the birds, and we decide to walk to the Chevron and treat ourselves to root beer. We usually stay on the cart path when we walk, but this time we veer across one of the long flat stretches of grass. And in the middle of that tall grass, we suddenly step into a huge patch of clover, as solid and dark as a big green swimming pool. Without a word we pull off our sandals and start wading barefoot into the field, the clover so cool and silky under our feet. I watch the clovers peek up between my toes, and I can't help kneeling down in them and running my fingers over them. I start counting the leaves, hoping, when I hear Lydia yell.

"I found a four-leaf one!" she exclaims, and I look over and see she's sitting cross-legged on the ground.

"Me, too!" I say, because as soon as she says it, I spot one myself. And next to my four-leaf clover, I see another four-leaf clover. And another. We keep looking and realize that about half of these clovers are four-leaf ones—it must be the luckiest spot in the world. We pick a handful each, but there's really no point to hunting for them. It's no challenge. But more than that, the only reason to pick a four-leaf clover is to make it yours. To claim it. We don't have to claim these lucky clovers—they're all ours. The whole wavy green field is ours. All of Lodema is ours.

We never make it to the Chevron for those root beers. We unpack our lunches in the middle of the clover field, and I lick ham sandwich off my hands as I bury my toes in clover. Lydia pulls off long strips of cheese and drops them into her mouth. I savor every one of my strawberries, and when I notice an ant crawling over my finger, I set her down near a bread crumb. She seems pretty excited about it. I watch her tear off a bread chunk and carry it off, making her way around giant stems and leaves that must seem like a forest of redwoods to her. When you watch an ant for a while, the world seems like an enormous place.

"Do you think a day seems longer to an ant?" I ask Lydia.

"Because it's smaller than us?" asks Lydia.

"Maybe," I say. "I mean, an inch seems longer to them. Maybe time is sort of like distance. It all seems bigger when you're tiny."

"I think they probably have no sense of time."

"When we were smaller, time went slower," I say. "Remember how long the summer used to seem? Or how long one afternoon could seem? When we were in kindergarten, nap time took forever. And holidays felt like they lasted for years. Now everything moves faster."

"Would you rather it move slower?" asks Lydia.

I think about that. Normally I would say no. I spend most of my life wishing for time to pass as fast as it can, hoping I'll speed along from one grade to another and finally be a grown-up, free to go wherever I want and do whatever I want. But sometimes when we're out here with the wind blowing and the baby birds *eep-eep*ing, I wouldn't mind if I could stop it all and just sink into one perfect moment like a fizzy bubble bath and stay there for good.

"That would be a cool power to have," says Lydia, like she's reading my mind. "The power to freeze time. To make one single second last as long as you wanted. Like the first bite of homemade ice cream or a Krispy Kreme donut. Or sliding down a waterslide and sliding and sliding and sliding and never stopping."

"Or rolling down the hill at Hole Six," I say.

Lydia starts to say something else, when we hear a rustle in the grass off to our left. It's so quiet that I think it's the wind at first. But the rustle is coming closer, and it's not a steady sound like the wind. It's uneven and clumsy and sounds suspiciously like someone walking—no, stomping—through the grass. And then I hear a few words of a song.

"No matter how hard a prune may try, he's always getting wrinkles," sings a high voice. *"A baby prune's just like his dad, 'cept he don't wrinkle half so bad."*

It's a kid's voice. A little kid, singing with total confidence like you do when you're in the shower. Lydia and I look at each other and don't move. I guess neither one of us knows where to go. And as we sit there, not making a sound, a little boy bursts through the tall grass into our clover patch.

And then he screams. Loud. Like he's falling off a building or being attacked by bees. It's one quick, panicked *ahhhhh!* Then he takes a breath and screams one long word, and it's not a word we expected.

"Mo-ommmmmmmm!" he calls.

"It's okay," Lydia says, sounding as panicked as he does. "It's okay. Don't be scared."

"We just came to pick some clover," I say.

He stares at us, not screaming anymore, which is good. I worry that maybe he's just catching his breath to let loose again. I figure the kid is maybe six years old. He's got short dark hair and big brown eyes and round cheeks. He's wearing a Chicago Bulls T-shirt that's faded but clean. And he seems to be going out of his way to keep one hand hidden behind his back. I cannot figure out what he's doing in the middle of an abandoned golf course. Maybe he thinks the same thing about us.

"They're lots of four-leaf ones here," he announces, in a surprisingly calm voice. "I thought I was the only one who knew about them."

He knew about them? I want to take a second and think about what that might mean, but I'm too afraid that he might start screaming again if I don't keep him talking.

"We just found them today," I say. "I'm Nell and this is Lydia. What's your name?"

"Jakobe," he says.

"Are you lost, Jakobe?"

"No," he says. "Are you?"

"No," we say at the same time.

"It's okay if you are," he says. "Don't be embarrassed. I can show you the way out."

"Are you here by yourself?" I ask.

"Well . . . ," he says, then stops. "I'm not supposed to talk to strangers."

"That's a good rule," says Lydia. "But we introduced ourselves."

"I found you hiding in my four-leaf clovers," he says.

"We weren't hiding," I object.

He shakes his head. "You're still strangers. And Mom says not to answer questions about us."

"Why aren't you supposed to answer questions?" I ask.

"That," he says, wagging a finger at me, "is a question."

"He's got a point," says Lydia.

"You're not helping, Lydia," I say.

"I should go now," Jakobe says. He turns around, looking back over his shoulder at us like we can't be trusted. He keeps looking at us while he makes his way out of the clover.

"Where are you going?" I ask.

"Home," he says.

He wades back into the grass. There's the sound of crunching leaves and shifting grass, then there's nothing but the sound of distant birds and bullfrogs. Only when he's walking away do I get a good look at what he's holding in his fist—it's colored chalk. He's got a handful of green, blue, and purple.

As I'm thinking about where I've seen those colors, I hear another voice somewhere nearby. This is an older voice, definitely a woman, sounding a little worried.

"Jakobe?" she calls.

"Coming!" he answers. And that's all we hear for a long time.

CHAPTER 10
GOING FISHING

A couple of days later, we're still talking about Jakobe and the unseen woman. We haven't seen any sign of either of them again.

"You think they're gone?" asks Lydia, chewing on her hair. "You think we're really alone out here?"

"I don't know," I say. "Probably. I bet they were just out for a walk. Some lady and her son who live in the neighborhood."

We've been through this several times now. I will admit, as I'm drifting off to sleep safe in my bed at home, my mind drifts to what I would do if someone suddenly bursts in Marvin's door. Someone who isn't a six-year-old. But I don't tell Lydia this. I only think about that sort of thing when my mind is wandering away from me. I don't like to think of anyone else having discovered Lodema. It's my place . . . I mean our place. And that's that.

"We should get started," I say, emphatically. "They like the early morning."

"But . . . ," says Lydia.

"It's going to be too hot if we don't get started."

"Fine," she says. "Hand me a cup."

This is our first day of fishing, and I've been looking forward to it. It's not blazing hot yet, and the trees are casting long, cool shadows. I hand Lydia a plastic cup. She volunteered to take care of the bait, so she starts turning over rocks and logs looking for insects. I pull out the Swiss army knife Marvin gave me, and I size up the young willow trees around us. I choose a couple of promising branches—strong, but not too thick.

"So what are we going to do if we catch one?" asks Lydia, her hair falling into the dirt as she shoves over a piece of dead wood.

"We're going to gut it, and we're going to eat it," I say.

Marvin taught me to fish. For a while, we went almost every weekend. Not here, of course. Sometimes we'd drive to the lake and stop for boiled peanuts or corn dogs at our favorite gas station. Sometimes we'd go to a pond owned by some guy he knew out Highway 280, and we'd buy fruit at Al's Farmer's Market and eat it without washing it off.

Marvin always said he was going to buy me my own pole. He left before he ever did. Or I guess we left. Marvin had a house on Red Mountain, and Mom and I moved in when he and Mom got married. I had my own bedroom in the basement, with my own television and my own CD player. I could hear Marvin's heavy, steady footsteps over my head late at night; they were the last sound I heard before I fell asleep. Sometimes I think about walking over to check if Marvin's still living there, but I'm not sure which would be worse—to see him there, sitting at his kitchen table without us, or to not see him there at all.

Marvin was—is—an engineer, but I think that's a waste. He should have been a teacher. He loved explaining anything— how the engine of the car works, how to spot Orion and the Big Dipper and a bunch of other constellations, how to bait a hook. When I caught my first fish, he rubbed the top of my head so hard that I got dizzy and nearly dropped the pole. He cheered and whistled while I reeled it in to the bank. When I cut my fingers trying to get it off the hook, he took the line from me and slipped the fish off as easy as pulling a roasted marshmallow off a stick. It flopped on the ground, and I would have felt a little guilty except that Marvin was grinning and trying to give me five with his slimy, bloody fish hands and calling me Little Nell, which no one else has ever called me before or since him.

Sometimes I miss being called Little Nell. It's like she only existed for as long as Marvin was around, and they vanished at the same time.

Even though Marvin had his own pole, and half the time I would use his, we always cut down a second pole. It was part of the ritual. Now I fold my knife up and run my hand down the two fresh-cut pieces of wood—they're smooth and cool.

I reach into my pocket for the fishing line.

Marvin left me three gifts when he and Mom split up—at least I like to think he left them as gifts, not that he just forgot about them. The knife was definitely a gift. He gave it to me the last Christmas. And on our last fishing trip, he'd stuffed a roll of fishing line and a pack of hooks into my backpack. I tried to hand them back to him when we got home, and he said, "Keep 'em for next time."

I think that means they were a gift.

So this is the next time. Only Marvin isn't here. I tie a piece of fishing line on the tip of each pole, where I've notched a little groove with my knife. I measure out the line and snip it off between my teeth, then run it through the hook.

I practice casting a little and nearly hook Lydia's ear. This could be a huge mistake because by now she has a cup full of beetles and grubs and earthworms. Dangerous ammunition.

"Are you sure this is a good idea?" she asks, taking a few steps away from me, but not reaching for any beetles. "Have you ever done this without Marvin?"

I don't really feel the need to answer that. Instead, I hand her one of the poles.

"It's not that hard," I say. "I just need to warm up a little."

"I don't even really like how fish taste," she says.

I look over, careful where I swing my pole, and notice that her lips are slightly purple. Her teeth are stained bluish, too. Mine are probably just as blue. We had blackberries for brunch. The vines grow thick along a fallen tree by the pond, and the berries practically burst when you pick them. My fingers are stained with them, under my nails and in the creases of my knuckles.

"You'll barely taste the fish once we fry it," I say. "It'll taste mainly like batter. Come on, practice casting."

I practice swinging my own line far out over the water, making a slow curve in the air and then waiting for the satisfying *plop* of the hook into the pond. I wait for the ripples to disappear, then I jerk the pole and bring the hook swinging back toward me. Then back out into the water, smooth and gentle. I relax into the rhythm and listen to the birds chatter. There are options other than fish, of course. Marvin had a couple of rifles, and he loved to hunt—deer, quail, sometimes even squirrels. I never had any interest in hunting. I won't kill anything I think is adorable.

Once we feel comfortable—Lydia masters a good cast quickly—we take a good look in her plastic bug cup. I pick up one of the grubs and work it onto my hook. Lydia watches me, opts for a worm, and baits her own hook.

"These aren't bad," she says. "Slimy, but not scary."

"You didn't mind looking under those logs?" I'd actually thought that finding bugs might get to Lydia. It'd be comforting to see her scared of something.

"There were a few spiders," she says. "But it's interesting, you know? Seeing what's under there? Under every log, there's this whole little world. And we never even know it's there."

"Huh," I say. I bet she wouldn't say that if there'd been roaches under the logs.

These ponds haven't been fished in a long time—maybe never—and it takes all of thirty seconds before I feel a tug on my line. That first bite is just an overgrown koi. It's like a goldfish meant for a very big bowl. I toss him back. As he hits the water, Lydia shrieks. She's got one. It's bending her pole into the water, so I can tell it's better than an overgrown goldfish. She lifts the fish out of the water with a jerk of her pole, and I grab it. It's a bream. A decent-sized one, longer than my hand.

When you're catching a fish every five minutes, fishing is very exciting. Not very challenging, but exciting. There's a breeze blowing over the water, rays of sun are filtering through the trees, and every so often, a fish gleams silver as it breaks the surface. Lydia laughs every time she gets one on dry land.

I think of long summer days in the apartment, listening to Mom's steps to figure out which room she's in. Sometimes I can tell her mood by the sound of her high heels. She slams her feet down on the wood when she's angry. Sometimes it's not worth leaving the apartment because, before I can get through the front door, I have to get past her and talk to her. And talking can go very badly. When I'm trapped in my room, I try to make the time go faster, watching each minute tick by: 11:01. 11:02. 11:03.

Now I breathe in the wide-open air, and I think the sky is a shade of blue I've never seen.

By mid-afternoon, we have over a dozen good-sized bream, more than enough for us and Saban, too. If we just had ice and a cooler, they'd keep for days. As it is, we need to eat them this afternoon. It'll be a feast.

I pick up the first fish, my thumb in his mouth. He's not moving anymore. I grab him by his tail and hold him against the inside of a plastic cup. I use the edge of a spoon to scrape the scales off him, moving from his tail to his head. They glitter in the bottom of the cup. Next I stand him on his stomach, like he was swimming. I pull out my knife again, and I hold him with one finger in his gills. Then, slicing behind the gills and slanting backward, I cut off his head.

I could never do anything like this to a bird.

I run my knife inside the fish and scoop out everything we don't want to eat. The whole process takes about five minutes. The nice thing about bream, Marvin told me once, was that they're too small to fillet. When we caught bass, they'd have to be sliced open and the bones removed; it was twice as much time and effort.

Marvin's stuck in my head now, clinging like the fish scales on my hand. For once, that's not such a bad thing. Usually when I think of him, I feel heavy and empty at the same time. But with my hands busy and scaly and slimy, remembering him makes me happy. I feel like Little Nell again. I work my way through the pile of fish, slicing and cutting and tossing heads into the grass, and if I close my eyes—which is a bad idea when you're using a knife—I can imagine that Marvin is next to me, casting out into the pond.

"Saban's eating a fish head," says Lydia.

I look over. It's true, and it's not pretty.

"Well, I'm not taking it away from him," I say.

Lydia yells, "Drop it, Saban!" a few times, then gives up. He looks at us suspiciously and drags the fish head a little farther away.

I pile together leaves and twigs and get a little fire going. While I wait for it to get hot enough, I arrange a little cast-iron skillet, a bowl, a bottle of oil, and bags of cornmeal and flour in front of me. I go through the motions just like Memama taught me: First, make a mix of half flour and half cornmeal. Next, swish a fish around in the mixture, getting it good and coated. (Memama dipped the fish in milk and egg first, but dairy products aren't very convenient here.) I feel the meal and flour underneath my fingernails, gritty like sand.

I pour oil in the pan and set it over the fire. When I start to see tiny bubbles, I toss a fish in. I hear the same sound sizzle whenever Memama's frying okra or potatoes or eggs. It's the same sound the corn-bread batter makes when it hits the hot pan.

As I lay the fish in the pan, it strikes me that even though I'm thinking of Memama, I'm not exactly missing her. It feels like she's nearby, almost within sight just like Marvin was a minute ago.

"You're quiet," says Lydia.

"I am not."

"You are so."

"I'm just thinking."

"Are you missing home?" she asks.

"No," I say, surprised. "Of course not. Are you?"

"A little."

I hardly even hear her. I feel more at home right now than I have since the last time I was curled up on Memama and Grandpops's couch. I've got Marvin and Memama looking over my shoulder.

I focus on the sound of bubbling oil. I think I'm close to realizing something, or connecting something. Something related to Memama or Marvin or both. There was some thought rolling around in my head that was worth holding on to. It's like trying to remember the lyrics of a song—I'm close to getting it, but it won't come.

I do have the sudden thought that Lydia said she was a little homesick.

I look over at her. "You're home every night."

"I miss air-conditioning," she says. "And television. And all the food in the refrigerator. And my dad's supposed to get home this afternoon. I do sort of like coming down the stairs when he walks in the door."

I watch the fish. It's browning on the bottom—I flip it over with the end of my knife. I finish cooking it without making any more conversation. When it's done, we nearly burn our fingers pulling it apart. It's flaky and hot and crunchy with the cornmeal. We eat until we can't eat anymore—Lydia says this is way better than fish sticks—and we split a pack of raisins for dessert. Saban gets three fish all to himself.

When we stand up to head back home, we don't bother putting our shoes on since it's a short way, and we've worn a path through the grass. We hold our shoes in our hands and swing them as we walk.

"You know what we should bring tomorrow?" Lydia says, licking her fingers. "Wet wipes. My hands still taste like fish."

She sounds more upbeat than she did earlier. Maybe she was just hungry. I feel good, too. Full and happy. I've got a leftover contentedness that might be as much about Marvin and Memama as it is about the food.

"Are you okay with being here?" I ask Lydia. It's a question I couldn't bring myself to ask her when she sounded homesick.

She swings an arm around my shoulder. Her hands do smell like fish.

"Sure," she says. "It's our biggest adventure so far, isn't it?"

CHAPTER 11

A VISIT DOWN UNDER

Late one afternoon, we're playing a game of slapjack in Lydia's rocket ship, sitting in the chairs of the blinking control panel. Just when my hand has turned a deep shade of pink and Lydia's a few cards from taking the entire deck, there's a knock at the door.

A knock at the door. Of the rocket ship.

Saban growls under his breath, edges toward the door, and then starts barking his head off. We don't try to shush him.

"Hello?"

It's a woman's voice. Saban barks even louder. He's practically vibrating.

"There's no lock on the door," whispers Lydia.

I swallow. My mouth is suddenly painfully dry. My tongue feels twice its normal size.

"Is it the same voice we heard before?" I ask. "With Jakobe?"

"Maybe."

Saban has shifted into a low, constant growl. I think this voice could also belong to the police or to whoever actually owns the golf course. This voice could be about to tell us that we're spending the rest of the summer at a home for juvenile delinquents.

"May I come in, girls?" the woman calls again. She knocks more softly.

Lydia's off the bed before I can stop her. She scoops Saban up in her arms, stalks to the door, and throws it open, holding Saban in front of her like a shield.

The woman at the door is small, and she's smiling. Her hair is short and mostly gray and shining in the fluorescent lights.

"Hi," she says again, calmly, like we're walking into her classroom on the first day of school. "I was hoping to introduce myself."

I walk as quickly as I can to the door, standing next to Lydia so that our shoulders are touching. Together, we're blocking the door. This woman doesn't seem threatening, but, as Jakobe says, you shouldn't trust strangers.

"My name is Gloria," the smiling woman says. "I live at Hole Nine."

"You live at Hole Nine?" I repeat. I'm so close to Lydia that her hair is tickling my chin.

"For now," the woman says.

Lydia and I look at each other. Surely she can't be serious—if someone were living around those empty aquariums, we would have noticed by now.

"May I come in?" Gloria asks again.

We both step back. I don't move my hand from my pocket. She moves past us, perfectly relaxed, and—in a way Memama would very much approve of—gracefully lowers herself into one of the spinning seats. She cocks her head at the looks on our faces.

"This would normally be the part where you tell me your names," she says.

We do.

"It's nice to meet you," she says.

Then we stand there a while longer and stare at her. She smiles back and twists her chair from side to side.

"Please don't look so stunned," she says. "You don't have anything to be nervous about. Yes, I live here. And you've already met my son."

"Your son?" says Lydia.

"Why didn't you talk to us then?" I ask.

"Well, honestly, I've been hoping that the two of you might give up. I thought you'd get bored and go away."

She makes it sound like we're in preschool. Like we might wander off after a shiny toy.

She holds her hands up in an apologetic way: My annoyance must show.

"No offense," she says. "Anyway, it looks like you're not going anywhere. And we all need to make the best of it. We've only seen you during the day—are you here at night, too? Have you run away from home?"

"No," I say quickly. "We go home at night."

"So your parents know you're here?"

"Umm," I say.

"Errrrr," says Lydia.

Gloria studies us. "So you'll be staying for how long?"

"For the summer," says Lydia.

"Well, welcome to the neighborhood," says Gloria. "Would y'all like to see our place?"

"You mean your putt-putt hole?" asks Lydia.

"Same thing," says Gloria.

We're confused and a little suspicious, but she seems friendly enough. Even sort of charming. And what are we going to say? No, we do not want to see how you've been living right next to us in underground aquariums without us even knowing? Yeah, right.

We follow her out the door, and she makes small talk as we walk. She points out the bird nest at the top of an old light pole, and she tells us that the sprinklers come on every night at ten minutes past midnight. She has no idea why there are still sprinklers when there's no one around to pay the water bill. But if we're looking to take a good shower, she says, ten minutes after midnight is the time to do it.

We come to the stairs leading down into Hole Nine, and, even in the afternoon sun, I can see a faint glow from the bottom. At our feet, I see the small curved shapes of the three openmouthed fish. As I watch the back of Lydia's head bob down the stairs in front of me, it occurs to me that this could be some sort of trap. Gloria could have anyone down here waiting for us, hiding in the shadows and ready to spring. It would have been smarter to bring Saban. He's a nuisance, but he knows when strangers are around.

But the bottom of the stairs looks exactly as we remember it—empty aquariums, some bits of coral inside, lots of dust on the glass, and those painted symbols. I can't see any signs of life. No criminals hiding in wait. No snakes weaving in and out of human skulls. Also, no beds or blankets or anything like furniture.

"You stay down here?" Lydia asks Gloria.

"Not exactly right here."

Lydia has stopped by the painted symbols again. She runs her finger over the purple circles. "Did you paint these symbols?" she asks. "Do you know what they mean? Is there something below us? Did there used to be tadpoles down here?"

Gloria cocks her head like she can't decide what to make of Lydia. Teachers sometimes give Lydia that same look— when she answers a question in class, she usually shouts out three or four answers at once, just to make sure she gets the right one.

"I painted them," says a voice behind us, and I know it's Jakobe before we turn around. "And they're not tadpoles."

He's standing behind us, leaning against the glass. He's got a half-eaten apple in one hand.

"You painted the same signs on the tree where we climb into Lodema, didn't you?" I ask, even though I'm sure of the answer. "And you did the chalk drawing on top of the castle."

"Yeah," he says.

"So what do they mean?" asks Lydia.

"I paint the best things," he answers. "My favorite things about here. The green means rolling down the hills, and the purple is the blackberries, and the blue is the sprinklers at night."

"Why those things?" I ask.

He takes a bite out of his apple. "Because they're my favorite. What else would you paint?"

I study Gloria again, her old jeans and clean gray T-shirt, and her eyes with smile crinkles in the corners. I notice that Jakobe's wearing the same Chicago Bulls shirt he was wearing the other day.

"You're . . . homeless, aren't you?" I say.

Gloria shakes her head. She has silver earrings with little silver feathers dangling from them. They make a sound like bells.

"We've just hit a rough patch," she says. "We'll be leaving soon."

"We could stay here forever," says Jakobe hopefully.

"I'm glad you're enjoying yourself," Gloria says. "But a golf course isn't quite the same as a house. Now come on, girls, you haven't met the whole family yet."

She turns and walks to the second set of stairs, the ones we'd used to exit the aquariums and climb back aboveground.

"I think Lodema is much better than a house," I whisper to Jakobe. He looks pleased.

Instead of walking up the stairs, Gloria walks around them and stops at a dark corner, where I see nothing but shadow. She reaches toward the wall—at least it looks like a wall—and with a small movement of her hand, she opens a door. Soft light pours out of the door, and we hear someone say, "You back, Mom?"

"It's me," Gloria says. To us she explains, "This is an old

maintenance entrance. When they needed to clean the tanks, they'd drain the water and then the cleaning crews could go in through this door."

She steps inside the door, and we're right behind her. As soon as we step through the doorway, we're surrounded by aquarium glass again.

When we first came down here, we thought we were looking at two aquariums, one on our left and one on our right. But they aren't two separate aquariums at all. It's one big U-shaped aquarium—the two sides we can see from the staircases are joined by a glass tunnel that runs behind the walls. This back section is completely shielded from view.

Unlike in the exposed parts of the aquarium, there's no dust and trash back here. The floors are swept clean. There's a sofa, a little refrigerator, and a couple of lamps. The orange glow of the lamps reflect off the glass walls. There are three twin mattresses with blankets and pillows on them. Against the back wall, the glass is wallpapered in posters. It's square after square of pictures—the Eiffel Tower, an astronaut on the moon, a hummingbird drinking from a flower, a tiny island in the middle of a turquoise ocean, New York City, Mohammed Ali, a baby dressed up like a flower. It doesn't look like you would expect a bunch of random stuff thrown together underground to look. It's colorful and warm and cozy.

"This is our place," says Gloria. "Nell and Lydia, this is my daughter, Maureen."

One corner of a wall has a spigot on it, the kind where you could attach a garden hose. There's a girl washing a dish in the stream of water. She stands up and grabs a towel as we walk in. She's tall and thin and looks like she's in high school.

"Hey," she says. "So you're the girls Jakobe met at the clover patch. Mom said she was going to see if she could find you."

She walks over to us, flipping her short black hair out of her eyes. It's cut like a boy's, but with loose curls that flop over her forehead. Her skin is very pale and smooth like a piece of drawing paper.

"Nice to meet you," I say. "It's really cool down here."

Maureen shrugs. "Mom's good at decorating. She can always make something out of nothing. And that's pretty much what we've got."

"We've got lots of stuff, Maureen," says Jakobe with a frown.

His sister ignores him. "How long have you guys been coming here?" she asks us.

"About three weeks," I say.

"Why?" she asks, a little bit of a challenge in her voice.

"Because we like it," says Lydia, a little bit of annoyance in her voice.

I jump in before Lydia can say anything else. "So how long have you been here?"

"Too long," Maureen says. "Since March."

"I don't think it's too long," says Jakobe.

"And it's not permanent," says Gloria.

"It feels like it," says Maureen.

First of all, every time Maureen says something, there's something about the tone of her voice that isn't exactly rude, but it's, well, not quite friendly, either. Second of all, I get the feeling this is a conversation that the three of them have had plenty of times already. I see Gloria give Maureen a warning look, a sort of be-nice-while-the-guests-are-here look.

Maureen turns back to us. "How old are you anyway?"

"I'll be thirteen in October," I say.

"So you're twelve," she says. "That means you're twelve."

I feel Lydia tense up beside me, and I suddenly know exactly how to describe the tone in Maureen's voice. It's like at the end of every sentence, she's silently adding *"and you're probably an idiot."* Gloria is flashing the warning look again. I know Lydia is close to calling Maureen an idiot (or something worse) out loud—Lydia's not big on patience. But I keep my tone cheerful. I am the salesclerk announcing something over the intercom; I am the hostess at the restaurant asking how many people will be at your table.

"Yeah," I say. "Twelve. How old are you?"

"Seventeen. I'll be a senior in the fall," she says. *And you're probably an idiot.*

"I'll be in first grade," says Jakobe, tapping my arm. His finger is sticky from the apple. "I won't have to take naps anymore."

I'm glad Jakobe is here. He has better conversation skills than his sister. But something happens to Maureen's face when she looks toward Jakobe—it gets softer. Her mouth relaxes and the wrinkles in her forehead go away. For the first time since we walked in, she smiles.

"You never took naps even in kindergarten," she says.

"I had to fake them," says Jakobe. "Fake naps are worse than real naps. More boring."

"Jakobe is a man of action," says Gloria. "You might have noticed."

Jakobe shrugs like he is very aware that he's a man of action. He takes a few steps and hops on the sofa, tucking his feet under him. He seems very comfortable there, very at home. Part of me is impressed by what they've built here. And part of me, I admit, is disappointed that somebody else came up with the idea of living on a golf course. I thought I'd been really original.

"How did you pick this place?" I ask Gloria.

"I used to come play putt-putt here when I was a teenager," she says. "I lost my job at the beginning of this year, and after a while, we couldn't pay the rent anymore. It was a, well, stressful time. Somewhere around then it seemed like checking out the old golf course might be a fun break from, well . . ."

"Life," Maureen interjects.

Gloria laughs, and it's a pleasant, startling sound. It makes you want to laugh, too.

"Life," she agrees. "I brought the kids here one day, and we sneaked in to see what had happened to the place. A little adventure. And the more we snooped around, the more I started thinking that this could be a lot better than sleeping in our car at night. A free place to stay until I can find us something better."

"And that is how we came to live in an aquarium," says Maureen, but the corner of her mouth is turning up now.

"An awesome aquarium," says Jakobe.

"Couldn't you get in trouble for being here?" asks Lydia.

I do not think it's one of her sharper questions frankly. We could *all* get in trouble for being here.

Maureen sort of snorts and opens her mouth to answer, but Gloria puts a hand on her daughter's arm before she says anything.

"Actually, the possibility of getting in trouble is one reason I came looking for you," says Gloria. "To get you to be more careful."

"She means that you need to quit stumbling around all over the place in the broad daylight," says Maureen. "Making noise. Coming and going all the time. You're going to blow everything."

"I don't know what you mean," I say.

"I mean you're going to ruin this for us," says Maureen.

"Maureen . . . ," warns Gloria.

"They will, Mom," she says. "I may not want to live here, but it's all we've got."

"Hey, you're the ones who came to find us," says Lydia. "We didn't even know you were here."

"You'd already run into Jakobe," says Gloria. "You were bound to figure out we were here."

"But why would that matter?" I ask. "Why are you so worried?"

"There are occasionally maintenance people here for fallen trees or power lines or sewage system problems," Gloria says, running a hand through her hair and making it stand up like a hedgehog's. "Sometimes people from the city check out the property. You're right out in the open, and there's always the chance you'll get caught. If that happens, we don't want you to lead them to us."

"We don't want to get caught, either," I say.

"But if you get caught, you just go back home," Maureen says. "If we get caught, it's much more complicated."

Once again, silence. And more silence. I think I hear a single cricket playing a little tune somewhere in the aquarium.

CHAPTER 12
OUR DOG IS SERENADED

At first it seemed like packing bathing suits had been wishful thinking. Most of the ponds here are disgusting—muddy brown with a thick scum of algae over the surface. We call one Dead Man's Lake, another one Mucous Lake, and a third one Mutant Alligator Lake. (The best fishing is at Mutant Alligator.) But the fourth pond, over by Hole Twelve, is pretty and pale green and free of algae. Go-for-a-Swim Lake. As you wade in, you feel soft moss squishing between your toes, but the water itself is clear in your hands.

Lydia and I are doing the backstroke side by side. The sun is baking our faces. I feel a fish brush my leg as I kick.

"I'm going to touch the bottom," Lydia says.

She dives, and I watch her turn into nothing but a whitish blur underwater. When she comes back up, she's holding a clump of dark green from the bottom of the pond. I liked it better when I didn't know what the algae actually looked like up close.

I float on my back while she treads water, and for a while, the only sounds are splashing. I think Saban is chasing grasshoppers. We haven't seen anyone else out here for a couple of days.

I think about how if we actually lived on the golf course, we could take baths here. I'd bring shampoo and conditioner, and the suds would float across the pond. I don't think the fish would mind much. It would be a huge, mossy bathtub. But at the moment we just swim and dive and feel the tiny silver fish weave around our legs.

Our feet get filthy as we tiptoe back onshore—the mud seeps between our toes and the grass sticks to our wet skin.

"Wanna splurge today?" Lydia asks. "A bag of chips? All I have is peanut butter and jelly and an apple from home. Mom needs to go to the grocery store."

The longer we've been here, the more free food we've found. The blackberry bushes are nearly done blooming, but we've found a couple of plum trees and a half dozen fig trees. And there's always the fish, of course. It'd all be enough to live on, really, even if we didn't have supplies from home. We'd get sick of fruit and fish, but we could do it. If we needed to. When you think about it, we'd have everything we need here—food, water, a place to stay. It would be possible.

But Lydia's right—chips do sound good. Better than figs.

We usually treat ourselves to some gas station snacks once or twice a week. I've seen the cool girl at the cash register once more. Her name is Alexia. That's all I know. Last time she was wearing earbuds and suggested I listen to something called "Disco Inferno."

"Where's Saban?" Lydia asks, pulling on her shorts.

"I don't know," I say.

We call for him, and, of course, he's nowhere to be found. I swear, there's a part of me that thinks I should have written that Camp Elegant Earth would not allow dogs.

We call him again and again, listening for any sign of him—a bark, a rustle in the weeds, a splash in the pond. Lydia yells that she'll give him a treat, and even that doesn't bring him running. We wander for five or ten minutes, starting on the bank of the pond and working our way farther out into the bushes and the willows and oaks.

"Saban!" Lydia calls again. "Saban! You want a bone?" (She doesn't actually have a bone, but Saban doesn't know that.)

We keep walking and calling. Briars tear a long scratch up the side of my calf, and I watch a thin line of blood appear. Mosquitoes have discovered the back of my neck, and they think it's delicious. I slap at them again and again, but more keep coming. All of a sudden we hear barking, then growling. Then what seems like singing. I look toward the sounds, and through the trees, I see Jakobe's dark head. I hear him laugh and, as I make my way closer, he turns toward me. He has a white puffball in his arms.

"You want him back?" he asks.

"Yeah," I say. "How'd you catch him?"

"I sang to him," he says.

"You what?" I ask.

Lydia ducks under a tree branch and runs over to Saban. Jakobe hands him over, and she kisses the top of his furry head before she glares at him. "Bad dog!" she says. "No treats. No treats."

"He wouldn't come to us at all," I say to Jakobe. "What did you sing to him?"

He shrugs and takes a breath. When he starts singing, it's the tune to "Row, Row, Row Your Boat," but he's changed the words.

"Come here, little dog, come over to me/
I will scratch your belly good and teach you archery."

"Archery?" I ask.

"Dogs like rhymes," he says. "A lot of animals do. I can get birds and squirrels to come to me, too. Not cats, though. They aren't musical."

He's kind of an odd kid.

"What are you doing out there?" I ask. "Just singing to animals?"

"Nope," he says. "I was looking for you two. Do you want to come over to our place and visit? It's nice and cool. You don't sweat at all in the aquarium."

Lydia and I look at each other, then back at Jakobe. He looks hopeful. I bet he gets bored out here all by himself, no other kids around.

"Thanks," says Lydia. "But I don't think this afternoon works."

"Mom said I could invite you," he adds, like maybe that was the problem. "She says you can come have lemonade. She makes really good lemonade. It has cherries in it."

You can tell by his voice that he's impressed by his mom. Maybe everybody's impressed by their mom when they're six years old.

"That sounds great," says Lydia. "But we've got some stuff we'd like to do today."

"Like what?" he asks, looking back and forth between us.

"Exploring," I say. "Checking out some things."

As soon as I say it, I can tell he'd like to come with us. I can see him think about inviting himself along, and I wouldn't blame him if he did. I'm almost sure I couldn't turn him down, not with him looking at me with those big eyes. But he doesn't ask. The hope fades out of his face, and for about a second he looks disappointed. Then the disappointment is gone, and he grins.

"Okay," he says. "Maybe tomorrow."

"Maybe," I say.

"And thanks a ton for finding Saban," Lydia says.

I can tell she feels a little guilty, too. We don't really have a set plan for today, although we always wind up exploring one way or another. The truth is that we like being on our own. That's why we're here. We came to Lodema to get away from family. And now there's this whole new family—a family that lives underground in an abandoned house for fish, that is—and they're sort of invading our space just by being here. It feels like we should set some rules, draw some boundaries. I don't want to be rude, but I'm not really interested in being best friends with Jakobe. No matter how adorably odd he is. Or how cute and chubby his cheeks are.

He doesn't seem to need our company anyway. He's tromping through the grass again, paying no more attention to us than if we were a couple of turtles he thought might be entertaining until we refused to come out of our shells.

"Hey, Jakobe!" I call.

He keeps swishing through the grass. "Yeah?"

"If I were a bird, what would you sing to get me to come to you?"

He stops. "What kind of bird are you?"

"Does that matter?"

"Sure."

"Mmm, okay. I'm a sparrow."

"Are you sitting out in the grass, right in the open? Or are you hiding?"

"I'm hiding," I say. "Under a bush."

"All right," he says, narrowing his eyes. "That makes a difference. Some birds are easy—they just want to play. They want to be entertained. The hiders need more than that. They need to know why it's worth coming out."

The kid has clearly thought about this.

"Okay," he says. "So you're under the bush. You're a small bird, but fluffy. I can hear you cheeping. . . ."

He swallows a couple of times and leans in closer to me. I feel like he's about to reach out and touch me even though he's still ten feet away. Lydia starts to giggle, but I can barely hear her over Jakobe.

"You have soft feathers . . . and small blinky eyes," he sings. It's to the tune of "On Top of Old Smokey," and his voice is clear and sweet. *"You think you're safe if you stay in disguise/ But you can't fly if you stay where you are/So come out and see if you can land on a star."*

Lydia's not giggling anymore. She's smiling, but it's a friendly smile.

"I'd come out for that," I say.

"I don't think birds can really land on stars," Jakobe says, "but I also don't think they know that. It sounds pretty good, doesn't it, to tiptoe around on one? I bet they'd be fizzy."

For the rest of the afternoon, I wonder every now and then if Jakobe is singing any birds out of bushes. If you'd asked me a month ago to name some talents, I'd probably have said dancing, painting, sports, baking . . . stuff like that. But out here at Lodema, there are different talents. Jakobe singing animals out of hiding places. Gloria transforming an underground aquarium into a beautiful apartment. Lydia's coyote howling and bug finding and algae diving.

At first I just thought there were amazing things inside Lodema. I'm starting to realize that, actually, there are amazing things inside of people. Maybe all the wide-open space here makes it easier for those things to come out.

It's getting harder and harder to come home every day. I'm usually climbing the fence and walking through the Wasteland just as the sun is going down, and as the light disappears, so does life at the golf course. It's started to feel like my real life, and my life in the apartment is the fake one. The dream one. The apartment is mostly in the dark, with a black sky outside, and Lodema is in bright light all the time. I'm definitely awake there. I can see everything. Things get cloudier at home.

Tonight when I step into the apartment, I see three boxes piled on the kitchen table. That means one thing: board game night. Mom loves board games. Not the word ones, like Scrabble and Boggle, which I usually win. She doesn't like the strategy ones, either—like Battleship or Labyrinth, which I always win. She likes board games that involve acting or singing or charades or drawing spaceships that everyone thinks are hats. She likes being as silly as possible.

"I never did grow up," she says, grinning.

"No, Mom," I say, because I know that's what she wants me to say.

We play a game where you look at a word, then you draw a picture of that word, pass it to the next person, and that person guesses what the picture is supposed to be. You do that until you've passed it all the way around the table, and usually the final guess is nowhere close to the real word. Usually you'd want to play with more people, but we don't need to because Mom is an absolutely terrible drawer. Seriously. She draws a cow, and you think it's a spider; she draws pigtails, and you think it's a squash. Once her word was "lemonade" and Lionel's best guess was "a baby."

She's also a terrible guesser, although I think she's bad on purpose sometimes.

I pick up the drawing pad and turn to my original phrase.

"This was a piñata." I show my fairly decent drawing of a hanging piñata and some kids hitting it.

I turn the page. "And Mom guessed . . . a zoo? You guessed a zoo?"

"There are kids looking at an animal," she says. "A horse. Or a zebra."

Lionel has already cracked up.

"No, they're not," I say. "There are kids hitting a horse with a stick."

"Rough zoo," says Lionel.

"They could be feeding it," says Mom. "Feeding it candy canes."

We're all giggling now.

"Why would they feed it candy canes?" I ask.

"It's Christmastime," she says, and she throws her tiny pencil at me.

I guess I'll go ahead and admit it: One reason that things are cloudier at home is because not all the nights are bad. Some are pretty fun. Sometimes I go to bed smiling. It's easier, though, during the bad nights and the bad days, to think that everything is always miserable. It's simpler. If it's not always miserable, then you have to start thinking: If I get five good nights for every ten bad nights, does that mean I should be satisfied? Two good nights for every ten bad nights? Does it matter how bad the bad is and how good the good is?

And if it's not good enough, then what? What option do I have?

On good nights and bad nights, I look through my window and watch Marvin peering over the trees. If I was a strange little kid like Jakobe, I'd think that dinosaur was wondering where I was.

CHAPTER 13
HATLESS ACORNS

There's a huge oak tree on the edge of the putt-putt course, and the ground underneath is filled with fallen acorns and their hats. The hats are the top part—the stem part—of the acorn. At Marvin's house, there was an oak tree nearly as big as this one, and he parked his pickup truck underneath it most days. The bed of the truck would fill up with nuts, sometimes with the hats attached, sometimes not. And I'd go out there and sit in the middle of the truck and try to match up any bald acorns with their missing hats. It's rare that you can find a good fit—every acorn is different. Most hats are too small or too big. But occasionally you slide one on, and it's a perfect match.

I'm sorting through nuts now, sitting cross-legged on the ground, a root digging into my knee. Lydia has gone to check on the baby birds, but I find acorn-hat hunting relaxing. And a little sad. There's something lonely about an acorn with no top, its little round head unprotected. That's why it's so satisfying when I can pair it up with the right hat.

I've got a handful of hats in one hand and a pile of acorns

in front of me when I hear footsteps behind me. It's Maureen, her curly hair pinned back with sparkly blue clips, and she's holding a bag of M&M's.

"Hey," I say.

"Hey," she says.

I expect her to say something snarky about me playing with a bunch of nuts, but she doesn't. She looks a little uncomfortable.

"M&M's?" she says, holding out the bag.

I take two red ones and a yellow one and hand the bag back to her. She folds herself up and sits next to me, brushing the acorns out from under her. I crunch my M&M's and wait for her to say something.

"What are you doing with the acorns?" she finally asks. She says it like she's really curious, not like she thinks I'm probably an idiot.

"Trying to match them up with the right hat," I say.

She glances over the ground, taking in the hundreds of acorns and hundreds of hats. "Do you ever find the right one?"

"Sometimes," I say.

She picks up an acorn and studies it. Then she starts collecting hats in her other hand. We work silently. I try to stay focused on acorns, but I'm really confused about Maureen being here at all. First of all, she didn't seem to like me or Lydia at all. Second of all, she's seventeen. In my experience, high schoolers don't hang out with middle schoolers. They do not sit in the dirt and play under trees.

"When you came by our place the other day," she says quietly, "I was still a little weirded out that you two were here. I was embarrassed for anyone to know this is where we lived. And I guess it seemed a little unfair that you have perfectly nice houses, and you just come over here for fun. It felt like the fact that you're here, I don't know, makes fun of us somehow."

I think about that. It hadn't occurred to me that Maureen could think we would seem luckier that she was. I've thought about all she has—a cool mom, a funny little brother, total freedom, and an aquarium for a house. For a second, I get a flash of what she doesn't have: her own bedroom, hot water, a television, money to buy clothes or books or maybe even food.

"You don't think all that anymore?" I ask. "You don't feel like we're making fun of you by being out here?"

"Not most of the time," she says, cutting her eyes at me. "I'm only slightly weirded out now."

I nod. One thing that's occurred to me lately is that I don't usually have to make conversation. With Lydia, conversation just happens. I don't have to think about it. When I'm home, whatever I say is totally wrong about half the time, so I try to stay fairly quiet. I don't meet a lot of new people. So you put me face-to-face with Adam Cooper or Alexia at the gas station or a random seventeen-year-old, and I'm not sure how to talk.

"You don't need to be embarrassed," I say, because it's true.

"Right."

"You don't."

She raises both of her eyebrows and they make neat little semicircles over her eyes. "Do you know what I found in my bed this morning?" she asks. "A dried-up starfish leg."

"You did not."

"Oh yes. I mean, who else wakes up and finds pieces of sea animals under their blankets?"

"The Little Mermaid?" I guess.

We both grin. I notice she has chocolate on her chin.

"I showed it to Mom, thinking she'd laugh," says Maureen. "But she nearly cried. She's more embarrassed about this whole thing than I am. She thinks she let us down."

"Do you think that?"

"No," she says immediately. "I get ticked off and worried that everyone at school will realize we lost the apartment, and I hate not being able to get new clothes, and I miss having a bedroom of my own. But Mom's doing all she can. She'll find something else. She's right—this isn't going to be permanent. I know that. But sometimes I don't feel it, you know?"

I nod. Nodding silently is something I'm very good at.

"You know what Mom still buys?" she asks. "Even though we tear napkins in half to make them last longer and she can't buy Tylenol when she has a headache? She buys big jars of honey because that's what Jakobe wants when he has a sore throat. Or just when he's faking a sore throat. How could I stay mad at her when she's still determined to buy him honey?"

I wonder if maybe there's wild honey somewhere around Lodema. There seems to be everything else. Why wouldn't bees set up shop in a nice hollow log? I decide that the next time I see a bee, I'll try to follow it.

There's probably not much chance of finding a nice healthy bunch of wild Tylenol.

Maureen has found a hat for one of her acorns. She holds it in the palm of her hand proudly, then sets it carefully on the ground.

"You want to come have hot dogs with us later?" she asks. "We usually build a fire in one of the sand traps and roast them. They're pretty good."

I feel like I'm in a tough position. I want to say, "We can't come because we have to be home for dinner." But is it rude to mention home when she doesn't have one?

"We don't usually stay here past dark," I say instead.

She shrugs. "Mom thought that might be a problem. We'll eat early. Five o'clock? That'll get you home way before dark."

"Can I ask you something?"

"I guess."

I'm still trying to make this new Maureen fit with the old Maureen we met in the aquarium.

"Why are you inviting us?" I ask.

Her hair clips sparkle in the sun, and she digs the toe of her sandal into the dirt before she answers.

"I should say Mom made me," she says. "I should say it's all her idea and I'm only trying to be nice. Or that Jakobe wanted you over. Because he gets bored with just the two of us for playmates."

"But that's not what you're saying?"

"I'm bored, too," she admits. "I mean, my two best friends know Mom lost her job, and they know we moved into our car for a while. They think we're still bouncing around from our car to motels. No one else knows we're in trouble. But living out here sort of limits my social life. I can't really have people over to spend the night or watch a movie, and we don't exactly have a lot of gas money for me to go meet friends. So I guess I've decided you two might be better to hang out with than a kindergartner and a forty-five-year-old woman."

"Thanks," I say. But I'm starting to think Maureen isn't so bad.

It's only hot dogs, right? It's not like they're asking to adopt us. We can eat dinner with them tonight, be polite, and then tomorrow go back to our regular routine. It'll be something new. Jakobe and Maureen aren't the only ones who'd like to see a different face now and then. Maybe Lydia and I could use a little more company. And there's something else: I'm curious how they do it. I'm curious how they live here. I'm curious how they are together. I'm curious about what sort of family they make. We've explored everything else here—maybe Gloria and Jakobe and Maureen are worth exploring, too.

Lydia's not hard to convince about the cookout, mainly because she really likes hot dogs. It turns out that an old sand trap is a perfect place for a fire—there's no danger of sparks landing anywhere flammable, and you can just kick the sand over the fire when you're done. We all find our own long thin branch, and we roast our hot dogs until the skin is black and crunchy. We cover them in ketchup and mustard and eat them right off the sticks, one bite at a time. Then Gloria shows us how to roast figs—which are not good with ketchup, by the way—for dessert. The figs are sweet and hot and melty and taste like little fruit pies. They fall apart in our fingers as we take them off the sticks.

Jakobe hisses and jerks his hand away from a smoking fig. He glares at it. Then he starts singing to the tune of "Twinkle, Twinkle Little Star."

"Cool down, cool down, don't you burn my hand/Or I'll stomp you and bury you in sand."

"Did that help?" asks Maureen.

Jakobe pokes at the hot skin. "Well, no," he says, "but I haven't worked with fruit much."

As soon as he's done licking his fingers, Jakobe starts asking if Maureen will read him a book after supper, so we all walk back toward Hole Nine. Maureen and Jakobe disappear down the stairs. That leaves Gloria, Lydia, and me. I suggest I could go get my deck of cards from inside Marvin.

Gloria shrugs.

"I was wondering if y'all would mind, um, if I fixed your hair," she says a little timidly. "I used to do that for a living. Style hair. And you girls have great material to work with. Since Maureen cut all hers off, I haven't had anyone to practice on."

I can tell she's afraid we won't like the idea, that maybe we're too old to have our hair fixed. But Lydia loves for people to play with her hair. Gloria has barely finished speaking before Lydia's scooting near her.

I offer to go get a hairbrush and ponytail holders, and once I grab them from Marvin, I walk slowly back to the windmill where Lydia and Gloria are sitting. There are low wispy clouds, and they throw shadows across the ground. As Gloria's hands weave in and out of Lydia's hair, the shadows of tree branches move across their shoulders and arms.

I watch Gloria, her eyes focused on the braids she's twisting. It's funny: When I think about how I wish my mother would be, I wish that she was like this. I wish that she braided my hair, with her fingers light and gentle, never pulling or hurting. While she arranges my hair, she would talk to me and tell me things and I would tell her things and there would be laughing. That's one of the pictures I have in my head. I know it's dumb, and I don't mean for it to be there. But there it is.

Gloria catches my eye. I give her the ponytail holders, and I watch as she finishes her work. Her fingers move as fast and smooth as the shadows. When she's done, Lydia has the sort of hairstyle no one wears in real life—she's got at least a dozen long braids, twisted and looped together at the base of her neck. It's the kind of hairstyle you would wear to get married . . . or to be named queen of some small country. I catch a view of her face, her chin up and her long eyelashes dark. She doesn't look like a queen from England or Portugal or anywhere that exists today. She looks like some ancient princess used to people bowing down to her.

"And you, Nell?" asks Gloria.

I shake my head. "Mine isn't as pretty as Lydia's."

"Don't be ridiculous. You have beautiful hair." She reaches out and lifts the ends of my hair, holding it like she's weighing it.

I sit down at her feet and lose myself in the feel of her hands in my hair. It feels like I thought it might—gentle and distracting. I close my eyes.

Too soon, she taps me on the shoulder. She's digging through her canvas bag with one hand, and she comes up with a piece of a mirror.

"See for yourself," she says.

I angle the mirror to catch the light the right way. She's gathered my hair into one thick braid that starts at the top of my head and then falls to the side, over my shoulder. The braid's loose enough that curls have pulled free and fallen around my face. I have to admit, it looks good. I almost don't recognize myself with my fancy hair and the flickering light. My eyes are bright, the color of sky. I have a sudden flash of my mother—I'd like her to see me like this. Pretty. Unrecognizable. For this second, at least, in this fragment of a mirror, I could be someone else from a long time ago. I could be powerful. I could be someone who rode horses bareback. I might give important speeches and lead ceremonies.

"It's beautiful," I say, still looking into the glass.

"You're beautiful, silly," says Gloria. "You both are."

I lay down the mirror and hope she will not keep talking like that. It makes me feel ridiculous—Lydia is beautiful. The golf course is beautiful. When Gloria uses the word to describe me, I know she's just being polite. I finger the mirror's edge, worrying it with my fingernail. Gloria doesn't say anything else, and in the silence, I realize part of me did not want her to stop talking. Part of me wanted to hear her say it again. The mirror seemed to agree with her, even though it still doesn't feel like the girl in the mirror was me.

I scoot sideways and turn toward Gloria, who has leaned back, her palms flat on the concrete. Lydia has lain down flat on the fake grass of Hole One, separated from us by a narrow cement walkway.

"Gloria, why haven't you been able to find another job?" I ask. I want to touch my hair, but I'm too afraid of messing it up.

She sighs. "You want the long answer or the short answer?"

"Give us the short one first," says Lydia, sitting up.

"It's not easy to find one," says Gloria.

We wait a second.

"Okay, give us the long one," says Lydia.

"All right," Gloria says, and starts twirling the short hairs at the nape of her neck around one finger. "I spent months looking for work, applying to every job I saw listed. And then we ran out of money and couldn't pay the rent any more. So we moved into the car for a little while. And that changed things. To apply for a job, I need to turn in job applications. If they need to be typed, I need a computer. If I get lucky enough that someone wants to call me back, I need a phone number. So where do I get a printer? Whose phone number do I use? If I actually get an interview, I'll need nice interview clothes. I need, I need, I need."

Gloria rolls her head from side to side like she has a crick in her neck. Her earrings jingle.

"What about a homeless shelter?" asks Lydia.

"A homeless shelter would help me with the clothes," Gloria says. "They'd help me with phone calls. And I did stay in a shelter with the kids for a few nights when all this started. We were in bunk beds. And all around us women were snoring and tossing and turning and coughing and maybe vomiting, and I was desperately trying to sleep so I could make a good impression at an interview. I'd get a couple of hours of bad sleep, then I'd have to start moving about six A.M. And my kids were with me, exhausted, wandering around. We'd go back to the shelter at night for another couple of hours of sleep. Then we'd start another day where I'd hope someone would call, and they wouldn't.

"At least here we have our own space. We have our own rules. Jakobe gets to play and feel like he's got the biggest backyard in the world. I keep an eye on the listings in the paper, and I still apply for anything that looks possible."

"You can get unemployment, right?" Lydia asks.

"I don't have an address, sweetie. That's another 'I need'— I need an address. So, no, I don't get checks. We scrape by here. I have a little bit left in my savings. I sell my jewelry when I need to. I go to a food pantry sometimes."

"Could you go back to school?" asks Lydia. "Get trained for another job?"

"That would cost money," says Gloria. There's another jingle of her earrings. She looks at me.

"You're quiet, Nell. What are you thinking?"

I'm different than Lydia. When she doesn't understand something, she asks questions until she does. When I don't understand something, I turn it over in my head until it makes sense. I don't speak until my thoughts are still, because I don't want to say the wrong thing. I watch Gloria's face—crinkle lines around the eyes, wide mouth, sun-browned face—and one question comes to me.

"Are you happy?" I ask.

She looks up at the willow branches swaying in the wind. "No," she says. "But we're together. That's enough for now."

CHAPTER 14

CHANGING THE RULES

The main difference between the idea of living on a golf course and the actual fact of living on a golf course is that the idea only takes a few seconds. The actual fact lasts sixty full minutes of every single hour. You can only walk around and swim and fish and eat for so many of those minutes. And in this heat, trying to think of new things to do is exhausting. Usually at least once a day I wind up just lying on my back under a tree, staring up at the leaves. It's not exciting, but it's free and it's easy.

We've been here almost a month. Lately, when I'm staring at how the branches cut the sky into interesting blue shapes, I'm thinking about Lodema. I'm thinking about how Jakobe keeps talking about the sprinklers, about how fun they are at night. I want to see those sprinklers in the moonlight. Maureen said building a fire is much better at night, and of course it is. Fires are always better at night. Gloria says she has some really scary ghost stories, but, of course, she only tells them at night.

I remember the first night we snuck out here and how

weird and fantastic the putt-putt course looked in pitch-black with the glow of the lights coming out of Marvin and the rocket ship. When you think about it, it's a total waste that we're only here during the day, when nights are the most pleasant time. If we could just play all night and then burrow into the cool dark ground like moles or gophers and sleep all day long, that would be perfect. Claustrophobic and dirty, but still perfect.

I think I've figured out a way to make that happen. Not the gopher part, but the night part. We could go to sleep here and wake up here. It would be like we really lived here, like this was our actual home.

I find Lydia wading through the edges of Go-for-a-Swim Lake. She's watching the mud squishing between her toes. She looks up as I make my way through the weeds.

"How come when you cool your feet off, it cools off the rest of you, too?" she asks.

"Dogs have sweat glands in their feet," I say. "They cool off through their paws and their mouths."

"But we're not dogs."

"We're mammals. Dogs are mammals. Maybe that means something."

She kicks a spray of water at me. "Science is not really your thing."

"I want to ask you something," I say. "What would you think about your camp sending home a letter telling your mom that you're invited to spend the night at camp for a whole week? Starting next week."

"You mean I'd spend a week here," she says, popping a

piece of hair into her mouth. "Since camp is completely imaginary."

"Well, yeah," I say. "And, I told you, the camp is not imaginary. The camp exists. You're just not going there."

"And you'll tell your mom what?"

"That my summer school needs to have an intensive all-night study camp that week."

Lydia does not look that excited. She steps out of the water and makes her way to the Hut. I guess I haven't mentioned the Hut. That's been Lydia's project for the past few days—she said she wanted a house with a nice view. So she stuck a bunch of dead branches in the ground and made three walls. She used some kudzu vines and tied two branches in an X, criss-crossing them across the top of the walls. Then she piled fresh, leafy branches on top of the X to make a real ceiling. The leaves hang down over the walls and blow in the wind. You can see through the walls—it's like a house made of giant toothpicks—but it looks cool. It's what you might build if you were stranded on a desert island. I keep thinking she should be sitting in there eating coconuts.

Now she climbs into the Hut, brushing the hanging leaves away from her face. She pats the ground next to her, and I come inside, too. It smells like dirt and rain and grass.

"Why?" she asks, once I'm sitting down. "I mean, I'm not saying no. But why do you want to stay out here at night?"

"Because night will be so much fun."

"It's because you want to spend more time with them, don't you?" she asks, pinching a leaf off her ceiling.

The truth is that we have been spending more time with

Gloria and Maureen and Jakobe this past week. Sometimes we eat lunch or go for a hike. A few times we've spent the afternoon in the aquarium. It's a lot cooler belowground, and you can do a lot more with a group—more games, more conversations, more stories. I know Lydia likes Jakobe, and I'm pretty sure she likes Gloria. (I'm not sure about Maureen.) I also know Lydia has been unusually quiet while we're with them, and, honestly, I haven't wanted to ask her what's the matter. Because I think I know.

"Don't you like them?" I say finally.

"I like them fine," she says. "But I don't exactly want to move in with them."

"We're the roommates," I assure her. "Just the two of us."

There's a house on Clairmont Avenue, an old Victorian with gingerbread-icing trim along the eaves and a porch bigger than our whole apartment. It doesn't look so great now, but it could be beautiful. Lydia and I noticed it years ago and started to plan. We think we might live there under the gingerbread roof and stone chimney when we grow up—maybe during college if we go to college here in Birmingham, or maybe later when we have jobs.

Then again, we might move to New York and work as waitresses while we try to write a movie. We might get jobs on a cruise ship and sail from island to island, parasailing and scuba diving in our free time. We might move farther away: Lydia's Spanish is good enough to move to Madrid or Buenos Aires right now, but I'd need to do some serious practicing. We also heard that you can make a lot of money in Alaska. Alaska seems as different from Alabama as possible. If we went there, we would wear fur coats and be unrecognizable, just big bundles of cloth and fur with our breath smoking in the freezing air.

Lydia and I enjoy each other plenty now. But we plan to enjoy each other much more in the future. And there are countless futures out there, all of them a world away from our mothers.

"It's not that I'm jealous," Lydia says. "I'm not."

"What are you?" I ask, curious.

She thinks about it, ripping another leaf into tiny strips of green. "Surprised," she says. "You seem different out here."

"Different how?"

"I don't know," she says. "Farther away. Sometimes it feels like I just met you, and I don't know you at all."

First of all, I think that's ridiculous. Lydia knows everything about me. But second of all, if that were true, it would be sort of wonderful, wouldn't it? If you could turn into some new, exciting person? There's a part of me that wants to jump up and clap when Lydia says she doesn't know me. That's how I feel out here sometimes. Like I'm turning into someone new. Like I have amazing things inside me.

But if I'm someone new, am I still Lydia's best friend? I have to be. I have to be.

"I'm not different," I say to her. "You can still read my mind."

She rolls her eyes at me.

"I'm thinking of an object," I say. "Just one object."

She tries to fight off a smile for a while before she says, "Pepperoni pizza."

"Amazing!" I shake my head like I can't believe it.

She props her elbows on her knees and stops destroying leaves. She shrugs.

"You know, I really would like to see those sprinklers at night," she says.

That night, Mom meets me at the door with a spoon in her hand. On the spoon is chocolate icing, and when I take a long lick of it like it's a lollipop, the chocolate is so cool and sweet it makes my teeth hurt. It's perfect.

"Your favorite," she says. "White cake with chocolate icing."

"Thanks," I say, licking my lips. My favorite is chocolate cake with yellow icing, but I like this kind, too.

"And Grandpops and Memama are coming over for dinner."

"Great! I'll set the table." I clean every molecule of chocolate off the spoon. Mom doesn't bake much, and when she does, she uses mixes, which taste plenty good to me. (Memama would never use a store-bought mix for cakes, but she'd also never mention that Mom uses them. She'll act like she can't taste the difference, even though she can.)

"So what are you doing with your hair?" she asks.

"What?" I'm not sure what she means. The combination of the sugar and seeing Memama and Grandpops has me giddy. I've missed them.

"What's going on with those braids?"

I touch my hair. I've got two French braids, one on each side, and they meet together at the back. Gloria taught me how to do it. She said it showed off my cheekbones. "I like the braids," I say.

"Okay," she says, "It's your hair."

"So you don't like them?"

"Look," she says, coming back from the kitchen, drying her hands on her skirt. She kneels in front of me and puts a hand on each side of my face. She turns me one way and then the other like she's trying to catch the right light. "You choose your hairstyle based on what kind of face you have. That's one of the basic rules of beauty."

I have not heard any of the basic rules of beauty. But I'm sure Mom knows them all.

"Okay," I say. "So my face doesn't work with braids?"

"You get your face from your father's mother," she says. "You want to soften it some. Bangs. Layers."

Let me just say that I never knew my grandmother on my father's side. But from old photo albums, I would guess that she weighed four hundred pounds. She also looked a little— and this could be some technical glitch with old pictures— like a rhinoceros. (Memama's old pictures, on the other hand, show her lovely and delicate and smiling. Like a movie star. She was even prettier than my mother.)

Something tells me that my mother also thinks my father's mother looked like a rhinoceros. But I can't prove that.

My thoughts must show on my face, because my mother cocks her head and smiles at me. "She had a very interesting face. Distinctive."

A distinctive rhinoceros she means. I pull the hair band

from my hair and start untwisting my braids. My hair feels sweaty and tangled in my fingers. I'm not sure I can get it into a ponytail without needing to use a mirror, and I don't feel like looking in a mirror. I can tell how I look just by watching my mother's face, and all the joy of the day seems to drain out of me. Everything drains out of me— I'm not angry or disappointed or anything. I am empty. An empty rhinoceros.

But even though I rake my fingers fast and hard through my hair, the braids don't totally disappear. Soft waves fall around my face, like my hair doesn't want to forget the braids. I feel the S-shaped sections, and because my hair remembers, so do I. I think of Gloria's face. I think of how she makes a totally different kind of mirror than my mother does. I think of the actual shard of mirror she handed me, of how magical and powerful I looked.

That memory makes me turn around to the entrance hall, my hands still in my hair, where there's a small round mirror trimmed in silver. I look away from my mother and into the mirror and see myself with my own eyes instead of hers. And, honestly, it's kind of a crummy mirror. It's dusty and a little blurry, and I don't see the magical girl I saw reflected back at me on the golf course. But I don't see a rhinoceros, either. I see an out-of-focus face that might be beautiful or it might not be. I can see whatever I want to see.

I do not feel so empty. I feel a spark of something where the emptiness was. It's not a spark of anger or hurt feelings or misery, either. Mom has turned carnivore and attacked, and, for the first time, I don't want to attack her back or make her feel better or even disappear inside myself. What I want doesn't have anything to do with her. I want Lodema. I want the me that I've found at Lodema.

I follow Mom into the kitchen. I can only think about one thing. I can't wait any longer.

"Hey, can I stay at summer school overnight next week for a special study session?" I ask. "They're saying it would really help."

"Overnight for the whole week?" she asks, stirring the peas. "Even July Fourth?"

I forgot about July Fourth. Shoot. That's what I get for doing this on the spur of the moment instead of planning it better.

"Uh, right," I say, thinking she'll never fall for it.

"That's fine," she says. "Maybe Lionel and I will take a little trip."

And that's that. Clearly she's really going to miss me.

CHAPTER 15

WATER SPORTS

Three days go by. Our first night on the golf course, it's the lightning bugs that amaze us. We're coming out of the rocket ship, walking toward Marvin, and the course looks dark. Trees, bushes, hills—all pitch-black, nothing but outlines against the sky. Then I see something blink off to my left. I look toward it, and it's gone. But as I keep staring, I see another blink, then another. The trees are lit up with lightning bugs, flashing like strings of white lights. Hundreds, maybe thousands, of them. It's like our own private light show.

Then we look up, and there's a glow around the moon, a halo. Usually the moon is a clear-cut thing—a circle or a sliver pasted over black—but now it's all hazy at the edges. It's like the ghost of a moon.

This is what I learn on our first night: when you look carefully, you see things you usually miss. The longer we stare into the bushes, the more lightning bugs we see. When I stare at the downtown skyline, I see the red lights of a huge crane. There's so much here. Not just on the golf course, I mean, but in the dark itself.

"I'm glad we did this," says Lydia.

"Which part?" I ask.

"All of it."

There's thunder in the distance, very far away. That night I tuck myself into my air mattress with my pillow and old blue blanket, and I listen to the chirping and croaking and rustling outside of Marvin. And for the first time, I'm nervous. There's no lock on Marvin's door. There could still be snakes out here—we haven't proved there aren't. There could still be coyotes. There could be anyone out here. All that chirping and croaking starts to sound less friendly. I lie awake and stare at Marvin's ribs. I don't want to admit to Lydia that I'm too scared to sleep by myself out here.

So I count to one hundred, then to two hundred, then to three hundred. I'm wide awake. Then, because I'm looking for other things to count, I start counting Marvin's ribs. There are only twelve of them, but after I count the ribs, I start really paying attention to his heart and his lungs and the trails of veins all along his insides. I'm inside a dinosaur, I think to myself. I imagine I can hear his heart beating, and it beats along with the chirps of the crickets outside. My dinosaur. My bed. My golf course. And, eventually, I fall asleep to the imaginary sound of Marvin's heart *thump-thumping*.

Our second night, we decide to check out the sprinklers. Gloria told us the sprinklers come on at ten minutes past midnight, and she said the best spot was at Hole Seven. We've been hanging out at Hole Seven for nearly an hour—we wanted to scout out the territory before the downpour started. It wasn't hard to find the sprinklers: Lydia tripped on one of the metals heads sticking out of the ground as soon as we started wandering around. Now we're sitting near a whole row of sprinkler heads, all of them maybe ten feet apart. We're in the middle of a valley—a fairway—surrounded by the hilly greens of Hole Seven, Hole Seventeen, and Hole Eighteen.

"My legs really itch," says Lydia.

"I told you to wear pants."

"Why would I wear pants when we're going to run through sprinklers?"

"So your legs won't itch."

We already had this conversation once. I'm wearing Capri pants over my bathing suit, and I can't even feel the tall grass we're sitting on. Lydia is wearing nothing but her bathing suit. I think it's pretty clear who made the right choice.

"Is it time yet?" she asks.

"Almost." I check the clock on my phone. "Five more minutes."

"Don't fall asleep," she warns.

"I won't." I wonder if she's noticed that I've already fallen asleep twice. The sound of crickets is very relaxing. To keep myself busy, I break off a few blades of grass and start making a chain. I puncture the end of one piece of grass with my fingernail, then I slide the other end into the slit. It makes a loop. Now I fit another piece of grass through the circle, slit the end, and add a second loop to the chain. My record for grass chains before I came to Lodema was fifteen loops. My record now is 140 loops. That's what free time can do for you.

"What time is it now?" asks Lydia.

I'm about to tell her to make a grass chain when we hear a clicking noise. Then the clicking stops and there's a whirring sound all around us. Just as we look toward the sprinklers, water starts spraying from every direction. I gasp as a spray hits me in the eyes.

A shot of water straight in the face really knocks the sleepiness right out of you.

"Let's go!" yells Lydia, scrambling up.

We're soaked before we take a single step. My pants stick to my legs as I peel them off. My skin is cool, and when I start running, the breeze makes me even cooler. The water is waving over the grass in huge arcs, swooping toward us then away from us. It shoots at least a dozen feet in the air, giant sheets of water falling down in the moonlight. The water shines silver. I bet in the sunlight, we'd see some spectacular rainbows.

Lydia leaps straight into the water, trying to jump over it and instead getting sprayed from her feet to her head. I follow her. We run and jump and cartwheel and dive headfirst. The grass is so wet that if we get a running start, we can slide for several yards on our bellies. Then Lydia gets the idea to slide down the hills. We fall down at least a dozen times running up the hill for the Hole Seven green, then we flop on our stomachs and race each other to the bottom. We wind up in a tangled heap at the bottom of the hill, covered in bits of grass, laughing hysterically. Then we run to the top of the hill again.

It's sledding without a sled. And without snow. We call it sprinkler sledding.

Eventually we're sore and exhausted and panting for breath, so we go wash some of the grass off us in the nearest spray of water.

"How much do you want to bet me," asks Lydia, "that I can run from here to Hole Seventeen without letting the water touch me?"

"No way," I say. She'll have to go straight through the sprinklers to get to Hole Seventeen.

"I'll bet you a pack of M&M's," says a voice we can barely hear over the whirring sprinklers.

"Maureen!" I say, turning toward her. I can just see her silhouette; she's got a towel in one hand. Gloria is behind her—I guess Jakobe's in bed.

"You didn't tell me they were coming," whispers Lydia.

"I didn't know for sure that they were," I say. "I just told her we'd be here."

"Hi, girls," says Gloria. She drops her towel behind a tree and holds out her arms as the water swoops toward her.

Lydia sits down in the wet grass. "Is she camping with us?"

Camping is the second part of our plan. We've brought blankets to spread out under a tree. I did mention that to Gloria.

"Gloria, y'all didn't bring stuff to sleep outside, did you?" I call. She's holding her hair over a sprinkler head, and a curtain of water is dripping down. Her shorts and T-shirt are drenched. She sounds like she's spitting out water as she answers, "No way. We can't leave Jakobe for long. Maureen may stay longer, but I thought I'd cool off a little, wash my hair, and then head back."

"I'm glad you came," I say.

Lydia doesn't say anything. And she doesn't try to run to Hole Seventeen at all, not even for the pack of M&M's. She says she's gotten really tired. So I let her rest and let Gloria show me how fast sprinklers can wash the shampoo out of your hair. Then she shows me how to sit a few inches away from the heads, at just the right angle, and let the water massage my back. I watch the thin, smiling mouth of the moon, and I can feel the water pressure work its way up my spine, across my shoulder blades, then over my neck and head. It's like a thousand tiny fairy fingers, if fairies were massage therapists.

I try to get Lydia to join us, but she says she's drying off. By the time Gloria and Maureen leave, Lydia's already picked out a spot for us to sleep. I think maybe we'll talk like we usually do when we spend the night together, but her eyes are closed when I roll over toward her towel.

The next morning, I wake up when the sun is already in the sky. I nudge Lydia, who's already muttering and smacking her lips under her yellow towel. Once we've rubbed our eyes and woken up all the way, we gather up all our towels and start the trek back to the putt-putt course.

"You want to do this again tonight?" I ask.

"Maybe."

I try to read Lydia's face. "You don't want to go sprinkler sledding again?"

"It was okay."

I don't even know what to say to this. Sprinkler sledding is okay like ice cream and chocolate cake are okay or like roller coasters are okay.

I'm hanging my towel over one of Marvin's ribs when my phone rings. I've almost forgotten what it sounds like. I sit there for a second, wondering where the music is coming from. Then I snap out of it and reach into my pocket.

"Nell!" Dad says. "Your mother just told me you're in summer school. Why didn't you tell me? I thought you'd come over this weekend like usual."

Huh. I sort of forgot Dad.

CHAPTER 16

DAD

"Hi, Dad," I say. "I guess I forgot."

I have, at various times in my life, really adored my father. And I think there are times he really adores me. But those times never last very long. Dad has a short attention span. He promises to come for my birthday party, and he never shows up. He begs Mom to let him take me to hear Tina Turner when she comes through town, then he shows up twenty-four hours late. Once, years ago, when he picked me up on Friday, he told me how he'd found a turtle in his backyard, and he saved him specially for me. He talked about that turtle all the way to his house, how pretty he was and how I could name him anything I wanted, and how I could feed him lettuce leaves and change his water. Well, we got to the house and Dad had put the turtle in the drawer of his nightstand. I opened the drawer, and he was right—the turtle was beautiful. It had a brown shell with bright yellow markings.

It was also dead. Dad had forgotten to feed him.

I guess really it would be worse to be Dad's turtle than to be Dad's daughter.

Anyway, to forget about him in some ways is only fair. I'm supposed to stay with him every other weekend, but between traveling and working and girlfriends, usually he only wants me about half that time. I don't count on going over there unless he calls me first.

"You forgot?!" he says from the other end of the phone. "You forgot your own dad?! You're turning into a real teenager."

Dad loves to make jokes about how I'm a teenager.

"I'm sorry, Dad," I say. "I don't know how I forgot to tell you about summer school."

"Well, you can come this weekend," he says.

"Ahh, I don't think we have any free weekends. Rules and stuff."

He snorts. "That's crazy," he says. "What kind of school doesn't give you weekends off? And aren't you supposed to be a straight A student? Where did summer school come from? I think I'll just call the principal and see if he can't make an exception for you to have your regular weekend with me. Or maybe I'll come down during my lunch hour tomorrow—what's the address? Sometimes that works better, you know, to do things in person."

I hadn't counted on this. Dad's in an attentive mood. That's the thing about him—sometimes he really does pay attention. And he's really sweet and likable when he's paying attention. Even though eventually, you still wind up dead in a drawer.

In this case attention is not good. Not a single one of those questions was good. And there's only one way to answer them all.

"What if we do lunch tomorrow, Dad?" I say. "I can arrange it."

"You sure?"

"I'm sure. Meet me at John's City Diner at noon. I'll get a friend to drop me off. How's that?"

"Perfect," he says. "The more time, the better. You can stay after lunch, right? Spend the whole afternoon with me? You're not too old for father-daughter time yet, huh?"

"You want me to spend the whole afternoon?"

"I always want time with my daughter."

I can hear him smiling.

"Okay," I say. "I'll tell, um, them that I'll be out with you all afternoon."

At least seeing him will mean free food. I love the mac and cheese at John's. The steak and fries are also excellent.

I stare at the blank screen on the phone and realize I'm not just excited about the food. I wouldn't admit that, of course. It's just a thought that flies through my head, quick and skittish as a moth. Dad can be fun, really. We used to go for long walks, and he'd hold my hands and flip me over in midair. He knows a million knock-knock jokes, and the stupider they are, the funnier they are. Maybe we'll go to Railroad Park and walk around, and he can tell me the names of flowers. He's like an encyclopedia when it comes to flowers. We could go see a movie—we both like action. Or go wander around the bookstore—Dad likes books as much as I do. As I step outside into the breeze, I'm starting to feel very optimistic about my Saturday. Then Lydia peeks around Marvin's front leg.

"I'm baking out here," she says.

"It's hotter inside. It's at least two hundred degrees inside Marvin."

"You want to go for a swim?"

"Not right now," I say. "Maybe later. Gloria's gone for a job interview, and Maureen's going to the movies with a friend. I told them I'd watch Jakobe. I told him he could show me how high up in the oak tree he can climb."

Lydia's lifting her hair and swinging it from side to side, trying to cool off her neck. She doesn't say anything. I'm not an idiot—I know she's annoyed.

"We can swim later," I say.

Lydia drops her hair. "It was supposed to be us this summer," she says. "Our adventure. Like always. But it's not about us at all. I don't know why you even wanted me to come along. You'd be fine if you were just out here with Gloria and her kids."

"That's not true."

"You can't stay here forever, you know. You have to go back to real life."

I think of my tiny little bedroom in Marvin's rib cage, and I think of seeing myself in Gloria's mirror, seeing a version of me that I didn't even recognize. I want to see that girl in the mirror again, and so far she's not showing up in my mirror at home.

"I know I can't stay," I say. "You don't have to tell me that."

"Why would I tell you anything when you won't even listen?"

"What's the matter with you?" I ask.

Her shoulders slump, and her hair's damp against her

neck and shoulders. "Oh, never mind, Nell. Forget it."

"Forget what?"

But she's stalking away from the tree now, not even looking back. I nearly go after her, but I decide she's just miserable from the heat. She'll get over it.

The next day I tell her good-bye and start the hour-long walk to John's. My legs are stronger than they were a month ago, and I'm used to the heat. It's 101 degrees now, according to the digital sign by one of the banks, and I'm hardly sweating. I feel like I could walk forever, all the way to Alaska or New York or Buenos Aires.

I'm turning onto 5th Avenue when I catch sight of a silver car a couple of blocks away, turning toward me. It's Lionel's car. I know because it's a Buick with a bumper sticker on the front that says "WWSD? What Would Scooby Do?" I mean, how many of those bumper stickers can there be?

He's turned onto 5th now, and only two cars separate him from me. He's close enough that I can tell he's wearing sunglasses. I dive—actually dive—behind an azalea bush. A few hot pink flowers land on my knees. I think I'm hidden, but did he already see me? I listen for the sound of brakes, the sound of a car door slamming, the sound of footsteps. I wait, perfectly still, for as long as I can stand it.

All I hear is the *whoosh* of cars going past. I stick my head out and don't see Lionel or his car. Still, I'm shaken. All it would take is one person—Lionel or Mom or a neighbor—to see me, and Lodema would be over, finished. I'd be dragged back home, and I'd never spend another night inside Marvin or running through sprinklers. I start walking again, this time with my shoulders hunched and my face down. I wish I had a baseball cap or a scarf or some sort of disguise. I feel so exposed walking down the street now, like I might be snatched up any second, like the ripe plums we pick off the trees. I start to feel sorry for poor defenseless fruit.

Finally, I'm at the restaurant door. Safe. No one will snatch me in here. If we see anyone I know, Dad will say I'm just on a break from school.

I'm surprised to see that Dad is waiting for me. He's not usually too punctual. He holds the door open for me and then hugs me, warm and tight. I smile against his T-shirt. He's put on weight in the last few years, and the fabric is stretched tight across his belly. Every inch of his skin is covered in freckles, so until you get close to him, he looks like he's got a really good tan.

We sit down and order, and he gulps down half his glass of tea before he's ready to talk. To give him credit, he does let me talk first. He asks me about summer school.

"It's going okay," I say.

"You usually make such good grades," he says, and I think he might be about to ask me to tell him more about my life these days. To explain why I'm so different from the daughter he's always known. And if he asked me that question, if he showed me that he'd been paying attention all this time, I might give him a real answer. If he just asked me, I might tell him.

"Everybody has tough times," he says, taking another swig of tea. "I'm struggling a little right now. Bored with the job, you know. I'm on the road so much, and it's hard to eat right. I've been gaining weight, and my back's bothering me. But the worst thing is the new guy they've hired to run the office—he's twenty years old if he's a day. Complete idiot. Making my life miserable checking all my logs and calling up my customers."

Dad drives a truck delivering snack foods around the northern part of the state. He's been doing it a few years now, and he's never liked it. He tells me more about his boss and more about his back and then some about his cholesterol.

"It's high," he says. "Way over two hundred. They've been warning me about heart attack risk. I'm supposed to exercise. Supposed to eat more soluble fiber."

I nod and crunch on my ice as he talks. Our food comes, and the mac and cheese is phenomenal. It has prosciutto in it—I learned that word here at John's. It means sophisticated ham. I savor every bite of it as my father keeps talking. I finish my meal at least fifteen minutes before him because I've had nothing to do but eat, and he's hardly had a chance to take a bite. He's eating a hamburger, by the way, which can't be good for cholesterol.

"Ah, it's good to catch up with you, sweetheart," he says, finally, as he tosses his napkin on the table. I now know that Dad's boss is the nephew of the company's owner, that Dad thinks he has a wasp nest in his garage, and that Dad has started dating a woman named Brenda who collects unicorns.

I hand the waiter my empty plate. Dad's always been more of a talker than a listener. He probably needed to get that out of his system. I'm envisioning a stroll through the park where I can talk to him about *A Wrinkle in Time*. It's about a girl who meets three magical women—one of them used to be a star—and she's whisked away from her home to faraway corners of the galaxy so she can save her missing father. I've been trying to figure out whether she's disappointed when she comes back. It seems like it would be very hard to visit other planets and battle the forces of darkness and then have to go back to school the next Monday.

"So I've been reading this book," I say, propping my elbows on the table. "It's about traveling through the universe to other worlds."

"You ready to get out of here?" interrupts Dad.

"Oh. Sure. Okay." I wipe my hands on my napkin. "Where to now?"

"What do you mean?"

"Didn't you want to spend the afternoon together?"

"Oh," he says. "Did we say that?" He chews on his straw, picks his teeth with it as he looks at me.

I sink back into the booth. "Yeah. We did."

"I don't remember that. I thought we said lunch. I thought you were so busy with school."

I watch how the edge of his straw slides into the space between his front teeth. It's gross, but I can't take my eyes off it.

"That's fine," I say.

"I was planning on heading home, do a little yard work, maybe watch a game," he says. "But you could come with me."

"Right. No. You should go on."

"I just thought you'd want to get back," he says. "I mean, I would have loved to spend more time with you. It's just that I haven't had many free afternoons lately. I'm dying to lie around and fall asleep on the couch."

"It's okay," I say again. I think of turtles in drawers.

If fries would keep, I'd order a to-go box for Lydia. I think Dad is still talking, but I'm just thinking about to-go orders. Maybe I should have saved some mac and cheese. But how would we have heated it? I could have ordered her a club sandwich earlier—she loves bacon. I picture the menu in my head, even though I know it's too late to order anything else. I just want to focus on something. We stand, we walk, and Dad keeps talking.

Dad hugs me when we get outside. He gives great hugs— he's warm and solid, and his arms completely surround me. I close my eyes and inhale the slight smell of gasoline that's always on his skin.

"Love you, Nell," he says. The words are so easy for him, just like breathing. It's like he loves hamburgers and he loves the Crimson Tide and he loves Pepsi and he loves a good ci- gar. Love love love.

"I love you, Dad," I say.

He drops me off at the Piggly Wiggly, where I tell him I'm meeting a friend who'll bring me back to school. That leaves me with a very short walk to the golf course, but I'm not quite ready to go back yet. Even after the scare this morn- ing, I can't bring myself to go climb the fence now. I'd have to explain to Lydia that Dad didn't actually want to spend the afternoon with me, and even though she wouldn't be surprised, I just don't want to have to say the words. I decide to wind through the neighborhood a little. Kill some time. I pick a side street by the grocery store that leads to a web of tiny, crooked streets. I don't know anyone who lives back here. It should be safe.

I twist and turn until I pass one house with a steep yard and a set of concrete stairs leading up to the wooden porch. Alongside the staircase, there's a stone pig on each side. Sort of like some people have stone lions looking all threatening at the entrance to the property . . . only these are small pigs. Very nonthreatening. The pigs are unexpected, but what makes me stop is when I notice that there's a girl sitting on one of the pigs. When she turns to me, I nearly trip over a crack in the sidewalk.

It's the girl from the gas station. Alexia. She blinks at me a second, then takes her earphones out of her ears.

"Hi," she says, and the way she says it, I know she recognizes me.

"Hi."

"Come grab a pig," she says, waving me over.

I walk over and settle onto the empty pig.

"Do you live around here?" she asks.

"Sort of," I say. "I live around the golf course."

"Nice. We go there for fireworks on July Fourth every year. Hole Sixteen. We jump the fence."

I didn't know that. Geez, you think you're running away to an abandoned golf course, and you find out it's crawling with all sorts of people. I'll probably wake up some morning with Girl Scouts knocking on my door selling cookies.

"Who's 'we'?" I ask.

"Me and my boyfriend."

She looks like a girl who would always have a boyfriend. "What's his name?"

"This one? This one's name is Darren."

"Doesn't sound like you're serious about him."

"I don't get serious," she says.

She's still swaying slightly to some beat that I can't hear.

"Maybe I'll see you there," I say. The Fourth of July is in three days.

"You'll probably see me more at the Chevron now," she says. "I'm getting my own place. Saving up all the money I can. Forty hours a week."

"How old are you?"

"I turned sixteen last week. It's legal."

"You're not going to school anymore?"

"Oh, I'll go back. But I gotta get out of here first." She jerks her head toward the house behind her. "I can't take it. Why do you think I'm outside sitting on a pig?"

I stare at her house, at the dark windows and the begonias wilting in the flower boxes. I can think of plenty to say, but I'm not sure about the etiquette. Somehow saying, "Is your mother crazy, too?" seems like it might be a little rude.

"Good luck," I say instead.

"Hey, listen to this," she says, and she hold out her earphone. I lift the speaker to my ear and listen. It's a woman's rich, clear voice singing along with the strumming of a guitar. The music makes me think of islands, of sand and water. I can almost hear waves in the background, and I think the sound might be something Hawaiian.

I watch Alexia as I listen. She looks small and thin to me now, not nearly as flawless as she does behind the gas station register. I can see her clavicle bones poking through her skin. I think about her working all day behind the counter, hour after hour, taking money and giving change and swiping cards and stocking shelves.

"That's what I want to do, for real," she says as I hand back her music. "Sing. Record some songs. I got plans."

For some reason, the sweet rise and fall of the song has made me sad. It's playing in my head as I think of Alexia standing behind that counter.

"I should probably go," I say, stepping away from the pig. "But I'd like to hear you sing sometime."

"Uh-uh," she laughs. "I'm not doing any shows in the Chevron."

"You got any CDs?"

"Not yet."

"I get one when you do, okay? When you've recorded your first track?"

She rolls her eyes but seems pleased. "Maybe I'll see you at fireworks. Or at the store."

"I hope so," I say.

I can't get the song out of my head as I walk. I walk faster and concentrate on my footsteps, hoping I'll break the rhythm. When I get to Clairmont, though, the skies open up, and the feel of rain knocks every thought out of my head. It's the first rain we've had in weeks, and the drops fall heavy and hard, stinging my skin. In seconds, I'm soaked through my clothes.

CHAPTER 17
ELEPHANTS AND LONG MEMORIES

As I scale the fence and drop into Lodema, the wind picks up, and I see the trees bending and bowing toward the ground. The water runs into my eyes and into my mouth—it's warm and slightly metallic-tasting. I sprint the last few yards to Lydia's rocket ship, and I bang on the door.

No answer.

I slowly open the door, calling Lydia's name. The silence is unnerving—no Saban panting or barking, no whir of a fan, no squeak of Lydia coming down the stairs. There's nothing but wind and the patter of rain against the sides of the rocket.

"I'm back," I call. "Lydia?"

Nothing. I jiggle the door, opening and closing it until the overhead light flickers and brightens. It takes a few seconds to realize what I knew on some level as soon as I heard the silence.

There's no one here. There's no fan, no dog, no pile of clothes, no trace of Lydia.

I sit down in one of the spinning chairs, and I close my eyes. I turn slowly, letting my feet drag on the floor. I am pleasantly dizzy, floating. I am not here. I am nowhere. I am only spinning and spinning and I might never stop.

My vision is all blurry when I notice the sheet of paper stuck between the buttons of the control panel. It's a few lines written on the back of a receipt. It says:

I went home. I told Mom I got homesick at camp.

I think I'm done for the summer. Have fun. Let me know if you want to meet by the honeysuckle tree later.

Your roommate, Lydia.

It bugs me how in books best friends are always getting into fights. Serious, hurling-insults, swear-I'll-never-speak-to-you-again fights. I mean, come on, I'm not in preschool. I'm not going to get into a big dramatic screaming match with Lydia. That would be stupid. I don't even feel angry with her. I'm like an acorn, I think, and I had the perfect hat. But I lost it. That strikes me as almost funny, even though I know it's sad. But I don't feel sad. I say that to myself, moving my lips, *I don't feel sad.* I spin in the chair some more, and thoughts of acorns and sadness fly right out of my head. The only thing I feel is dizzy.

When I feel steady enough, I pull out my phone and type, "*Sorry you left. Miss you.*"

And a few seconds after I push Send, she writes back, "*Then come home.*"

I tell her I can't. I do miss her. But I can't go back yet. That's all I type for the night.

I wake up the next morning, and there's still pink in the sky. I throw on some clothes, grab my Swiss army knife and a couple of hooks, and start walking. I never want to taste fish again, but fishing is at least a way to keep busy. Without Lydia, I have to find the bait myself. I start shoving over logs, and pretty soon I'm not even looking for bugs. I just keep shoving. I like the feel of straining my muscles, the satisfying sucking sound when the wood finally pops free of the damp dirt and rolls over. Even when my shoulders get sore and my fingers start blistering, I keep flipping over logs.

I am still very good at disappearing. I can leave my brain and my body behind anytime I like and float away into a good book or an interesting map or a beautiful golf course. I can focus on acorns or logs and leave everything else behind. But here's the thing about disappearing: it works really well when you want to stop feeling, but sometimes you *need* to feel something. It's easier not to think about Lydia, to just concentrate on rolling over one log after another and block out how much I miss her. But part of me wants to miss Lydia. That's not even right—I don't *want* to miss her. I don't want to hurt. But I know I should feel this. I need to feel this. Because it's important. I have to feel it so I can understand it.

So I let the thoughts and feelings come instead of shutting them out. I do understand why Lydia left. She thought we came out here so it would be just the two of us. That's not even quite right—she came out here because I asked her. She came out here for me, because that's what you do when you're someone's best friend.

But something's happened to me since I came out here. It started when we went fishing for the first time, when I threw a cast and felt Marvin standing there beside me. When I tossed a fish into hot oil and could almost smell Memama's lotion in the air. Then there was Gloria and Maureen and Jakobe. Even though I'm by myself out here, I feel like there are people all around me. Some of them are really here, and some of them are just echoes of people. But even the echoes are real, if that makes sense. It's like I let go of my tiny bedroom in our dark apartment, and I let go of Mom, and once all that fell away from me—once my normal life fell away—I floated high and far, and I found a different view. I'm not sure what I'm seeing, but I want to keep staring at it until I figure it out.

When I first came out here to Lodema, Lydia was all I had. She was everything. Our friendship was everything. And now it feels like my world could be bigger than just me and Lydia. I don't know if that's a good thing or bad thing, but I want to find out. I miss her—I get a pain deep in my stomach thinking of her empty rocket ship—but maybe without her here, this new view of things will make more sense.

Part of me thinks that. The other part thinks I should run as fast as I can to Lydia's house and beg her to come back out here. Beg her mother to let us be friends again. Beg them both to let things go back to the way they were.

Life would be so much easier if you only felt one way at a time.

I've been rolling over logs for what feels like hours. I think my hands are bleeding. My fingertips are slick with something that doesn't seem to be moss or mud. But I'm shoving against the biggest dead branch yet—it's twice as big as I am. The wood is rough and knotted, and the sweat runs down my face and drips on the ground.

The log gives way with a groan, and I strain over each inch until I reach the tipping point. Then the dead wood falls backward with a crash. I can hear my own breathing, harsh and loud. I try to lift my arms over my head to stretch, and I can barely move them. I might have overdone the upper body workout. Maybe I should actually look for grubs and worms now.

I kneel and grab a twig to start sifting through the exposed dirt. But what grabs my attention isn't wiggly and slimy—it's hard and white. I wonder if I've found a large shell, maybe a chunk of granite. I scrape back the dirt, and the white shape gets longer and thicker. Maybe a baseball bat.

I brush more and more dirt away, and I realize there are more white shapes, lying close together, sometimes on top of each other. Long and thin, some of them. Short and thick, others. I keep going until I find one that's buried deeper than I can dig. It's as wide across as a refrigerator. It's curved slightly, and when I touch it, it's rough and smooth at the same time.

Only then do I admit what I've found: it's a pile of bones. Very big bones. Like dinosaur big.

I almost call for Lydia before I remember she's gone. My second thought is that I need to find Gloria. I need someone to tell me what to do. I mean, if you find human bones, you call the police. What about dinosaur bones? Who are the dinosaur police?

I stand up, starting to jog to the putt-putt course, but I can't help thinking of Lydia. I've just made a major scientific discovery, and she's probably still in her pajamas. She's going to be so jealous.

I can't feel any of the soreness in my muscles anymore. I am running fast and easy like an animal on the National Geographic Channel. My feet barely hit the ground as I sprint through the grass. Gazelles should stay out of my way.

Once I see the tidy greens of the putt-putt course, I slow down, heading for the aquarium. Gloria and Maureen and Jakobe take their time climbing up the stairs at Hole Nine at first, but then they seem to switch to a higher speed once they understand what I'm yelling.

We all hike back to my newly discovered burial ground, and all of them seem very confident that I have not found a dinosaur. Once we're looking down at the massive bones scattered in the dirt, though, I notice no one seems so cocky.

"Maybe it's a buffalo," says Jakobe. "Or a whale."

I do not think it's a whale. In Alabama. On dry land. But Jakobe's only six, so I cut him some slack.

"Woolly mammoth," says Maureen. She nudges one of the bones with the toe of her sandal. "I think you've got the skull of a woolly mammoth."

Gloria's been squatting by the bones, and, as she stands

up, her knees pop loudly. She laughs her loud, contagious laugh.

"It's not a mammoth," she says. "But you're not too far off. I think we've just found Miss Fancy."

"Miss who?" says Jakobe, taking his foot off the skeleton.

None of us has any idea who Miss Fancy is. I think "Miss Fancy" sounds like a Sunday school teacher in a funny hat. Whoever she was, Miss Fancy must have been a very large woman with a very large head. We all start asking questions at once, but Gloria insists we settle down before she'll tell us anything.

"You can't listen to a good story when you're standing up," she says. "If you want to hear it, you've got to sit down."

We circle around to the green at Hole Twelve, just barely out of sight of the bones. Gloria tells us she wants us to look down on the rows of houses surrounding the course. She says it's a story more about the neighborhood than about the bones. She arranges herself on the ground and tosses her head so her earrings jingle. We hush and wait for her to begin.

"Well, back in the nineteen forties and fifties, this wasn't a golf course at all," she says. "It was a resort, the kind with a big hotel and a casino and a dance floor and a huge lake where you could go boating."

"And a concession stand," I add.

"Right," she says. "The resort also had a petting zoo. It had rabbits and goats and all sorts of farm animals, but its main attraction was the elephant. Miss Fancy. Miss Fancy loved visitors, and she especially loved children. In fact, she loved children so much that at least once a week she would break out of her cage, go lumbering up Clairmont Avenue, and show up at Avondale Elementary School. Her trainers would find her standing in the middle of a crowd of children. The kids would be emptying out their lunch boxes and feeding her their sandwiches and cookies."

I imagine an elephant at school, chowing down on sandwiches. I bet Miss Fancy liked peanut butter best.

"Then one day, Miss Fancy disappeared," continues Gloria. "No one knows what happened to her. Her cage was opened, but the kids at the school hadn't seen her. Rumors started going around. Some people said she got tired of being caged, and she took off across the state looking for elementary schools. Some people said her handler was sick of being outsmarted by an elephant, and instead of letting her get out of her cage again, he took her into the woods and shot her. And other people said she knew she was dying and just walked off to die in privacy. I like to think it was the last one."

"And no more elephants after that?" asks Maureen.

"Not that I know of," says Gloria. "Miss Fancy was one of a kind. Soon after she died, the resort closed. The petting zoo was shut down. And most people forgot there ever was an elephant that used to roam up and down Clairmont Avenue. But the kids in the elementary school grew up and had children, and they passed along the story. So Miss Fancy lived on."

Maureen and Jakobe wander off to look at the bones some more. I don't want to see the bones again. I'd rather imagine Miss Fancy alive and hungry, plotting her next escape. I close my eyes and think of a sunny, breezy resort, filled with people and dancing and music, with an elephant very politely sidestepping across the dance floor.

The ground is still soaked from the storm last night, but I find a nice flat rock and make myself comfortable. I must fall asleep, because when I wake up, I'm alone. Above me, a squirrel vaults from one tree to another. I watch an ant crawl across my wrist. I'm still trying to sort out what was a dream and what was a true story when I hear footsteps—it's Gloria. She's carrying two big cups, and she hands me one. I scoot over on my plastic bag to make room for her.

"I was thinking that maybe now I'd ask you to tell me a story," she says.

"Okay."

"Tell me why you'd rather live in an old golf course than live at your home."

I take a slow sip of what Gloria handed me, and it's lemonade, sweet and tart and cool. There's a cherry floating in it. I look up, and all I see is sky. The squirrel is still practicing gymnastics in the pine trees nearby. Part of me thinks that I'd be crazy if I wanted to be anywhere but right here.

But I know she's not asking why I'm here. She's asking why I'm not at home.

"My mother doesn't really want me there," I say.

This is the first time I've said this. Lydia and I know each other—and our mothers—so well that we never really spell out how we feel about them. And I don't talk about my mother to anyone other than Lydia.

Gloria breaks off a few blades of grass and lets them fall to the ground. "Okay," she says.

I'm glad she doesn't say, "Sure, she does" or "All moms want their daughters." I've heard that a few times, back when I was younger and still occasionally tried to make a teacher or a friend's parent understand what it was like at home. It strikes me that maybe Gloria didn't get along that well with her mother.

"So where does she think you are right now?" Gloria asks.

"Summer school."

She laughs her roar of a laugh. "That's original. She hasn't come to check on you?"

I lean back on my elbows and wish the stars were out already. There aren't many of them, even on the clearest nights, either because of clouds or pollution or city lights. I think of Marvin showing me Orion's Belt. I think of my earliest memory, which actually has both my mom and my dad in it, together, laughing under the night sky. I don't know what was funny, and I can't remember if I was laughing.

Some conversations are easier at night.

"Living with her makes me so tired," I say. "I'm always watching, trying to figure out if she's angry at me. And even if I figure out that she is angry, half the time I have no idea why. There's this weight in the apartment, like the air is heavy. Pressing down on me. There's no room for me in there. Her feelings take up too much space."

"Are you sure you're being fair to her?"

Gloria has one hand barely touching the ends of my hair, twisting a braid so tiny that I can hardly feel it. I relax into the feel of her fingers, and I think about my answer. It's not the first time I've thought about it. At least a few times a week I wonder if I'm the one—not Mom—who's the problem. Maybe I am. Maybe I should be more patient with her. Maybe I should be more like she wants me to be. But I'm not even sure what that is.

There's one memory that's underneath every moment I spend with Mom, and I can't quite bring myself to say it to Gloria. It feels private—private for Mom, at least, like I shouldn't share it with anyone else. When I was maybe seven or eight, I heard her on the phone. I still don't know who she was talking to that night—maybe some old friend from high school, maybe even my grandmother. But she was crying enough that her voice shook.

"This isn't who I thought I would be," she said. "I look in the mirror and I can't stand to see myself."

The person on the other end of the phone must have said something. I stayed perfectly still in the hallway.

"I can't," Mom said back. "There's something wrong with me. I'm so unhappy, and I'm just stuck. It's hard to get out of bed, you know? It's so hard to just get dressed and get out the door in the morning. What's wrong with me?"

That's all. She hung up pretty soon after that, still crying. No big speech. It didn't shock me that Mom was miserable. What shocked me was that she didn't say she couldn't stand to see me. She said she couldn't stand to see herself. And for the first time, it occurred to me that maybe what she feels doesn't really have anything to do with me. Most of the time, it's just the two of us in a small apartment. So maybe there's no one else she can take it out on.

ELEPHANTS AND LONG MEMORIES

That's what I try to remember, when things aren't good. That it's not about me. It's about her.

Sometimes it's hard to remember that. I lean forward and wrap my arms around my knees. Gloria's hand falls away.

"My mother loves dolls," I say.

Gloria stays quiet.

"Somewhere in the basement of the building, we still have trash bags full of her dolls," I say. "Their lips are rubbed off, and they're missing legs and arms, but she still loves them. She told me once that when she was a little girl, what she wanted most in the world was to have a baby. So she'd have her own little doll, only it would blink and eat and sleep.

"And so she had me, and she loved having a baby. She loved dressing me up in all those little clothes and cute little shoes and hair bows. That's what she told me."

"That sounds like she wants you very much," Gloria says softly.

"She did then. At first. When I was maybe in second grade, I found one of those bags of dolls. I pulled one out, and I was holding it when she came in. I never really liked dolls, you know? They're kind of dumb. They don't do anything. Mom came in and held out her hand for the doll. I gave it to her. She held it up to her face. She touched its hair. And she looked at me and said, 'I wish you hadn't grown up. I could hold you and love you and dress you, and I was so happy.'

"I think that's what she wants," I say to Gloria. "She wants me to be a toy she can play with and then put in a garbage bag when she's done."

I stop then. The words tasted ugly in my mouth, but I'm glad I let them out.

"Well, a toy doesn't ask for anything," Gloria says. "It doesn't argue with you. You can't disappoint a toy. Plenty of people would rather have a toy than a real kid."

"You think?"

"I don't think you're the only one in the world with an unhappy mother. I don't think you're the only one in the world who isn't happy at home."

I think about this. I know Lydia isn't happy at home. That makes two of us. I guess Alexia makes three. But I walk past other homes, even other apartment buildings, and the lights are on and I see women walking past with plates and bowls of food. I see kids watching television. I see dads carrying kids up to bed. I see dogs coming outside to use the bathroom and then running back to the door to be let inside, wagging their tails. Those homes look like everything is going along perfectly.

"So you think I should go home?" I ask finally.

I hear her earrings rattle when she shakes her head.

"It's not about what you should do. It's what you have to do. You can't stay here forever."

Lately I've been wondering if that's true. I don't want it to be true.

"What if I don't want to go back?" I ask.

) CHAPTER 18 (
STOP, DROP, AND ROLL

I wake up on July Fourth convinced that Alexia was kidding about watching the fireworks from Lodema. I mean, everyone knows the city sets off a huge display every year—it must last twenty minutes—and everybody has their favorite spot to watch. I usually watch from Lydia's balcony. But surely I would have heard about people coming to the golf course. Gloria looks horrified when I tell her about crowds of people coming. She has no intention of having her secret blown for the sake of a nice view.

The hours pass. I stay belowground for most of the day—it's cooler in the aquarium than anywhere else on the course. I've started doing crosswords. Gloria gets a thrown-away paper every morning now. So every afternoon I do the puzzles. I've even gotten desperate enough to do the word scramble, which normally annoys me.

"I've gotta go check Hole Sixteen when it's time for fireworks," I say to Gloria by late afternoon. "Just to take a look. Make sure no one's there. And, hey, maybe if people are there, you all can come out."

"Yeah, Mom," says Jakobe, looking very interested. "Can we go?"

She shakes her head. "We'll just stay here. We'll have our own private fireworks show."

"I can come back and get you if people are there," I say.

"We're fine," says Gloria. "I think we'll just keep to ourselves."

I start out toward Hole Sixteen as soon as it's getting dark. I hear the people before I see them. Usually the only sound of chattering here is when a flock of geese comes through. That's what it sounds like when I'm getting close to Hole Sixteen—like a huge flock of geese milling around. But pretty soon I can see the shadows moving, and I can hear laughing. Geese don't laugh.

There are tons of people here. Well, dozens. Which is way more than I expected. There are entire families on blankets, with coolers and flashlights and strollers scattered all over the place. Red plastic cups are propped up all over the grass. Small circles of people are talking and occasionally grabbing at a passing child. I assume all of these people live around here, along all the roads running behind and around Lodema. It's a big neighborhood.

I don't really want to run into neighbors, so I try to stay quiet and still, just on the edge of all the activity. I'm partially blocked by a pine tree. I'm still deciding whether or not I have time to go tell Gloria and the others about all this when a ripple of excitement goes through the crowd. Everyone looks up, and I hear explosions in the distance. The fireworks are starting.

The sky is still and black when we hear the first bangs and pops echo through the air. Then ribbons of light shoot toward the moon—they transform into starbursts and purple swirls. Smiley faces spread out across the sky. Another burst of sound, and four spinning planets float toward us. The explosions are nearly constant now, and there's a wave of red and blue and silver. Then more spinning planets. A blue comet shoots up and arcs down. A pink blossom dissolves into bright pink rain.

The fireworks build toward the big finish. A golden spiderweb stretches across the sky. The web begins to break apart, and the gold flecks float away, looking like shooting stars.

There's applause then, and another massive explosion of planets and flowers and smiley faces. A little freckled kid starts crying. I'm turning around, hoping to see Alexia, hoping maybe Gloria decided to let Jakobe come after all, when I recognize a face in the crowd.

It's Adam Cooper. He's holding hands with his little brother, who I remember from Railroad Park. Adam's pointing at the smoke that's hanging like clouds in the air. I don't move, and I don't say anything. But maybe he feels me notice him, because he turns toward me, smiles, and gives a little wave with his free hand.

I blink. The golden spiderweb is burned into my eyelids.

"Hey," I say, walking over.

"You live around here?" he asks.

I nod.

"Makes sense," he says. "I guess half our school could walk to this golf course."

"Do you come here every year?" I ask.

"First time."

I can't help but notice a bunch of small boys off by themselves, playing with sparklers. I'm not sure how safe that is. We had that big rain, but it's been such a dry summer that the soil drank all the water up in a day or so. It wouldn't take much to start a fire, especially with all the wild grass and dead branches lying around Lodema.

"I like the planets," I say. "I haven't seen that kind before."

"Blue is the hardest color for them to make," he says with complete confidence.

"Really?"

"I read it somewhere. And in Japan they do fireworks in the daytime. They make the smoke into part of the performance."

I wonder how much National Geographic he's watching. "So you're kind of a fireworks expert."

One corner of his mouth turns up. "I prefer the term 'fireworks genius.'"

Just then I hear a scream—more of a squeak, really, from the boys lighting the sparklers. I see silver flames dropping to the ground. A fallen sparkler. It dies out quickly, but the one on the ground isn't the problem—the problem is that one of the boys is waving his sparkler high in the air now, not paying much attention to where the sparks are landing. Where they're landing, unfortunately, are in the branches of a dying willow. Those long, ribbony branches could work just like the wick on a candle.

"Hey," I yell. "Hey, kid! Hey, little boy! Hey, boy with the sparkler! No!"

I can just see that tree lit up like a torch. And if it catches fire, the whole golf course could burn to the ground. But the dumb kid hasn't noticed me. Adam, of course, has noticed me, since I'm jumping up and down and waving like a lunatic. He follows my gaze and frowns.

"That kid's an idiot," he mutters. We both take off toward the idiot, dragging Adam's younger brother behind us.

"You're gonna set the tree on fire!" I yell. Now plenty of the adults have spotted me, but that one kid is still oblivious.

"Where are his parents?" asks Adam, running full speed. His little brother's feet are touching the ground maybe every third or fourth step.

And, then, like the picture in my mind made it happen, the tree goes up in flames. Or at least a couple of branches. It's like in those old cartoons where someone lights a bomb, and you watch the tiny flame burn up the string, bit by bit, inch by inch. The flames gobble up the branches, and now, *now*, the kid has noticed.

This is where things get weird.

"Aggghhhhhh," yells the kid.

"Justin!" yells some woman who must be his mom.

"Call 9-1-1!" yells someone else.

The kid, Justin, unfortunately has: a) poofy hair, and b) no sense of direction. Still holding his sparkler, he turns and runs right *into* the tree, into the fiery branches. They're not long enough to burn his face, but they do drag across his thick, curly hair. His head is smoking, the tree is burning, and the sparkler is still going strong.

Two adults have reached the tree, and they both grab for the kid. One has a blanket that he's trying to cover him with. But the kid is panicked and quick, and he scoots through their arms. He's zigzagging toward the tree trunk now, scattering sparks everywhere, screaming his head off.

There's a carpet of dead leaves under the tree, and sparks are raining down on them. I think I see smoke rising from them like fog. Smoke is everywhere—leftover in the sky from the fireworks, rising from the tree branches, floating up in wisps from the dead leaves.

Everything is going to go up in flames.

I yell the first thing that comes to mind: "Stop, drop, and roll!"

And the kid actually does it. He must have had the same lesson I had in kindergarten. He immediately falls to the ground in a heap and starts rolling around. He rolls right over the lit sparkler and all those bright, scattered sparks. Maybe it hurts, maybe it doesn't. But he's much calmer when he sits up, dead leaves in his hair, panting. His head isn't smoking anymore.

Adam has reached the tree, and he helps a bearded man pat down the drooping tree branches with the blanket. The blanket looks scorched, but the flames die out quickly. Then even the smoke drifts away. It all takes maybe two or three minutes.

"I called 9-1-1," says one of the adults.

"No!" I yell. Maybe a little louder than I mean to. Because we really don't need the fire department snooping around the golf course. What if they head over to the putt-putt holes? What if they walk down the stairs at Hole Nine and see beds and a sofa?

Before I can go find which of those adults called the fire department, Adam leans into me. His elbow is touching my arm.

"Stop, drop, and roll?" he asks.

I shrug. "Didn't they teach you that in school?"

He seems to be trying very hard to keep a straight face. "I believe that, uh, you're supposed to do that if you're actually on fire. I'm not sure it's an approved way of putting out a sparkler."

"It worked, didn't it?"

"I'm not criticizing you. You might be kind of a sparkler genius."

I hear the sirens then, and I'm furious that I've wasted these few seconds. I'm not the only one who looks disturbed by the sirens—none of these people are supposed to be here. This is private property. I think it's occurred to most of the grown-ups that we've all totally trespassed and then set fire to a place that doesn't belong to us.

I see the flashing lights of the fire trucks—so many fire trucks!—through the trees. They've stopped on Clairmont. Now everyone's grabbing their things—I watch them streaming like ants toward the sides of the golf course that do not have fire trucks parked beside them. Instead of dozens of people, there are maybe ten still standing here, ready to face the consequences. I notice that the boy with the sparkler is gone, and so is his mother.

"Should we run for it?" asks Adam. And the thought of that is so appealing—to laugh and sprint and hide in the trees together. To have a big adventure, just me and Adam. On the run from the law. But if we leave—if everyone leaves—the fire department and the police will surely take a look around. Maybe they'll take a careful look around, so careful that they explore the putt-putt course. I can't let that happen.

"I can't," I say. "You should go. I'm gonna stay here and explain what happened."

He doesn't take a single step.

"I'll stay," he says. "It's no fun escaping alone. And it looks like my mom's waiting around anyway. She doesn't scare easy—she'll probably talk to the firemen."

I see bright lights bobbing through the trees, then I see three men in uniforms walking toward us, their helmets tipped back. They all carry flashlights. I have to get rid of these firefighters as fast as I can. No questions, no curious glances, no investigations. An idea flashes across my brain like fireworks, and I suddenly know how to make that happen.

I kneel down by Adam's little brother and tip his face up toward me.

"Uh, this is Thomas," says Adam. "Thomas, this is Nell."

I'm not looking for introductions. I study the kid's face a little more. No good. He's sort of surly looking. I scan the few people still standing nearby, and I spot a little girl with pigtails. Big dark eyes, dimples. Adorable.

"I need that little girl," I say to Adam. "Any idea who she belongs to?"

"Ah, she's my cousin," he says. "Almost everybody still here is related to me. I think my mom is the only adult who didn't take off."

"How do you think your cousin is at playing pretend?" I ask. "Like at acting?"

"You're going to have to give me more than that to go on," says Adam.

So I do. Talking as fast as I can, I explain my plan to him. Then we sit down next to his adorable cousin and tell her what she needs to say. I've just finished explaining when the three firemen approach our group. The three of us stand up and walk over to meet the firemen. One is big, one is bigger, and one is totally huge.

"We received an emergency call from a cell phone," says the big one. "Do you kids know anything about that? The caller said there was a fire on the Lodema golf course."

The huge one says, "We don't see any sign of a fire. If this was some sort of prank, that's a very serious offense."

He's looking right at Adam as he says the words "serious offense."

I step up, lifting up Miss Adorable. Her name is Lisa, and she is four years old.

"It wasn't a prank, Officer," I say, even though I'm not sure you're supposed to call firemen "officer." I look sternly at the four year old. "Lisa, do you have something to tell the man?"

"I had a sparkler," she says. Her eyes are so big that she looks like a cartoon.

The huge firemen suddenly looks less fierce.

"You had a sparkler?" he repeats.

"I did," she said. "It was a big, fat one. But I didn't mean for it to hit the tree."

She smiles, showing a missing tooth, and it occurs to me that she might have a future in Hollywood.

It's time for my part. "We didn't know she headed this

way," I say. "We didn't mean to come on the golf course. But she ran this way, and she's really much faster than she looks. . . ."

"Are you fast?" asks the big firemen. He looks hypnotized.

"Pretty fast," Lisa says.

"We just lost her for a second," I say, trying to make my eyes big like Lisa's and having a feeling it doesn't work the same way. "And the sparks started to catch fire, but then we put them out."

"You and your boyfriend were watching her?" asks the bigger one.

I'm glad it's dark because I can feel the pink spreading across my cheeks. "Aghhhh . . ."

"Yeah," says Adam. "That's right. We were watching her."

"Well you're lucky nothing worse happened," says the big one. "No sparklers allowed in the city limits."

"Next time we might have to take you to jail, little lady," says the huge one. But he winks at her. I know we've won then.

Pretty soon the firefighters leave, and we promise to buy Lisa an ice cream sometime soon. Actually, I promise to buy her a horse. Adam makes me downgrade it to an ice cream. She scoots back to the small remaining circle of people, and we watch the fire trucks slowly pull away.

"Oh," says Adam. "Looks like you're about to meet my mom."

I follow his gaze and see a slender woman with short spiky dark hair coming toward us. She's a fast walker. I will not have time to escape. She grins at me, then gives Adam a shove, shoulder to shoulder. She knocks him slightly sideways, and he gives her a little shove with his own shoulder. I watch his face to see if he's embarrassed by this.

"Hi, Mom," he says. He seems to be perfectly comfortable with his mother tackling him.

"What did y'all say to the fire department?" she asks. "I was just getting ready to come over and accept a fine. Or a ticket. Or whatever they do to you when you sneak onto golf courses."

She looks like she wants to ruffle his hair. Or hug him. But she doesn't do either. She sticks her hand out to me and says, "Liz Cooper. Adam's mom."

I notice she has dimples.

"I'm Nell," I say, shaking her hand. "It's nice to meet you. I go to school with Adam."

"Pleased to meet you, Nell," she says. "I'll let you two talk—I've got a dozen or so kids to round up. I'm hoping they didn't get any ideas about starting fires. They *seem* like the kind of kids who would start fires."

"She means my other cousins," says Adam. "And she's right."

His mother is weaving through the few remaining kids and teenagers still packing up their food and their drinks and their blankets. Adam watches her as she kicks a stray soccer ball out of her way. He smiles.

"You like her," I say. This has just occurred to me. It's not that I thought he didn't like her. I just hadn't thought about it one way or the other.

"Mom's okay," he says.

"She seems, um, nice."

I am not totally sure what you say about people's mothers. Other people's normal, friendly mothers.

"She's all right. She's really into fireworks. And she really wants all of us—my sister and little brother and me and my dad—to come together. As a family."

"I thought the movie night at the park was family time," I say.

"She really likes family time. I mean, it's . . ."

I look back at his mom, and she's rounded up another sibling or cousin of Adam's. His mother has her arm thrown around the girl's neck, and the girl is not resisting.

"It's all right," he finishes. "It's family, you know?"

"Um, not exactly."

He shrugs. "My family's not bad. They're the ones who know you. You know? You don't have to try. Like I got my wisdom teeth taken out last year, and my whole mouth swelled and I couldn't stop drooling. I had to carry around a towel with me to mop up the drool. Mom didn't care. My brother and sister called me a Saint Bernard for a few days, but they didn't really care. I didn't even try to keep the spit in my mouth. Family's, like, the ones who stick with you even when you drool."

I look back at the sky, which seems so empty now. I did not know that about family.

CHAPTER 19
TO STAY OR NOT TO STAY

Even if I didn't have my phone to tell me the date, I'd know it was nearly August. The blossoms are scattering off the crape myrtles every time the wind blows, falling like hot pink confetti. Spiders or worms or something must be infesting the hedges because there are cobwebs spun across them, making them look like they belong outside a spooky old house. The pink crape myrtles fall into the webs, though, and in the sunlight, it's beautiful.

I have three more days here before my remedial social studies lessons are over. Three days before, in theory, I should be going home for good.

Every other day Lydia and I meet at the honeysuckle tree at ten A.M. This morning I see her when I'm still twenty or thirty steps from the tree. She's sitting with her back to me, hunched over the grass. I think she may be hunting for four-leaf clovers.

"Feeling lucky?" I call.

"No," she says, looking over her shoulder at me. "If I felt lucky, I wouldn't need to find a clover."

I settle next to her against the tree trunk. Soon I hear the sound of plastic or aluminum foil rattling.

"Here," she says, and when I turn, I see she's holding out a crescent roll through a hole in the fence. I take it, and it's still warm against my fingers.

"I've got four," she says. "Leftovers from breakfast."

"Thanks."

"Sure."

"You miss me?" I ask, mouth full of bread.

"Of course."

"Come out on the course with me today," I say. "Just for a few hours."

She shakes her head. "You know that won't work. Mom will check to see where I'm going. She's home today."

I swallow. "I know."

"And I never liked Lodema like you do. Not really."

"I know."

She passes me another roll, and I gobble it up in two bites.

"Is your mom still mad at my mom?" I ask. "Is she going to try to keep us from seeing each other?"

"I don't know."

"That means yes."

She doesn't say anything.

"I do miss you," I say. "It was better when you were here."

"So three more days," she says. "Then you're coming back, right? You're not running away from home to live at Lodema?"

She's trying to keep her voice light, but she doesn't exactly sound like she's teasing.

I lick my fingers slowly. I stare out at the golf course.

"What if I did?" I ask.

"That's not funny."

"It's not supposed to be."

"You're coming back," she says, standing up now, turning to stare at me. "You have to come back."

Her shadow falls over me, and I turn toward her. I sit there, my hands in the dirt and the weeds, looking up into her green eyes. I don't want to stand. I don't want to see her more clearly. I wish she would turn back around. When she left, it was like the last thing connecting my old life to Lodema vanished with her. It got much easier to imagine not going home again. Or maybe I should say it got easier to imagine Lodema becoming my real home.

"I could stay gone six months," I say. "Then I could come back to school. I might make it a year out here. I don't think Mom would think to look for me so close. Gloria would be around. She'd help me if I needed help."

"Does Gloria know about this?"

I ignore her question. "Maybe I could make it three years, and then, when I'm sixteen, I could get a job," I say. "I could get my own place and go back to school then. You could move in with me. No parents, no rules."

"What are you talking about?"

"It's true. It could work."

I'm not imagining me and Lydia, though. For some reason, she doesn't fit. Instead I picture me and Alexia walking to work together, opening envelopes that have our paychecks tucked inside, eating sandwiches during our lunch break. It is a blurry image. And when I try to make Alexia's face come into focus, she looks tired and sad, not at all how I want to see her. Lydia speaks and the image shatters.

"No, it could not work," she says. "You can't live here for years. And no one's going to rent an apartment to a sixteen-year-old. You won't ever make up years of missed school. You'd blow your chance at a scholarship. You know that."

I don't know why she's being so difficult. She never has any solutions—she just points out problems.

"There's no reason I have to make up my mind in three days," I snap. "I'll make up something to tell Mom. And I'll take a few months to decide."

"She's not stupid. She'll report that you ran away."

"Only if she wants me back."

That only makes her pause for a second.

"Your dad will report it."

Now I do stand up. "Shut up, Lydia! Leave me alone. This isn't about you."

She tries to laugh, but it comes out more like a sob. "Of course it is. If it's about you, it's about me, too. How could you leave me here by myself?"

"I'd still see you," I say. But I look away as I say it.

"Nell, do you really want to be alone?" she asks. "Do you really want to do this by yourself?"

"I wouldn't be alone."

I know that's true. Whatever I decide, I will not be alone.

Lydia flexes and then tightens her fingers. "Look, you're right—it's not about me. Forget me. You really think you're going to be happy if you run away?"

"You really think I'm going to be happy if I go back to Mom?" I put my hand next to Lydia's, close but not touching. "Lydia, she doesn't even care. Does she get to be my mother no matter what? No matter what she does? Isn't there a point where I can say, okay, enough. You struck out. You're off the team. I'm now advertising for a new mother. Don't I get to decide at some point that I'm done being her daughter?"

"No," she says. "I don't think so."

"That's not fair."

"It sucks."

"I want to be done."

She smiles, but there's nothing happy about it.

"Do you?" she asks.

Lydia's fingers brush mine as she takes a couple of steps, pacing.

"So are you staying here?" she asks.

I know the answer, of course. I've known the answer for a long time, but I haven't wanted to admit that I know it. I can't stay. Of course I can't stay. But the thought of being shut in that apartment with my mother again, of having her moods weighing down on me every second—it's just unbearable. It's the only answer, but I can't stand it. I can't say it.

Instead I say, "Do you think maybe I could still advertise for a backup mother? Just to pick up the slack?"

"A backup mother?"

"Or maybe a few backups. Depending."

She pops a piece of hair in her mouth and chews for a second.

"You picked me for a sister," she says. "That worked okay."

When Lydia goes back to her house, I just start walking. Not back toward the putt-putt course. Not toward anywhere. Walking and walking and walking, following the fence.

In the beginning, way back in May, I thought there was a good chance we wouldn't make it through the whole summer out here. I didn't say that to Lydia because I wanted her to be as fearless and confident as she always is. But I wondered about wild animals and insects and heat and injuries. I thought any of those things might force us to go home.

But the problem isn't any of those exciting things I thought about—I haven't gotten attacked by a wild coyote or stung by a mutant bee or tripped over a rock and broken a bone. I don't need any medical care. I haven't even lost any weight that I can tell. It's not like some of the adventures in books I've read, where the heroine is wandering through jungles or deserted island or other planets, and there's a pit of fire or an evil talking snake around every corner.

The reasons I cannot stay here are not dramatic. They are boring and practical and disappointing. School and money and laws.

When I stop walking, I'm standing in front of Maureen and Gloria. I see Jakobe a little ways away working to find a good foothold in the oak tree. I sit down, crossing my legs. Maureen is shuffling cards, and I like to watch her make them blur together. She looks at my face, sees something there, and puts her cards down.

"You're going home in three days?" she asks.

"Yeah," I say.

We all sit for a long time. She picks the cards up again and starts building a tower. Two cards make a tepee, then two more cards make walls around the tepee. Then one card goes on top to make a ceiling. Then the ceiling becomes the floor for the next level.

When she's on the fourth level of her tower, she says, "You had to. You can't just vanish."

"Right."

"Part of me wishes you could stay," says Gloria.

"Me too."

"You'll come visit?" asks Gloria.

"All the time," I say.

I scoot closer to her and lean my head in her direction, hoping she'll take the hint without me asking. She does. I feel her fingers combing through my hair. I close my eyes and let my shoulders relax. I let myself believe, just for a little while longer, that this is my life. This is my place.

Over the next couple of days I find myself walking along the fence often. I listen to music and put one foot in front of the other. Soon I'll be on the other side of the fence, and there's something comforting about pacing along beside it, mapping it out, reminding myself it is there. There is life inside the fence and life outside the fence. Mom is on the other side of the fence—she's taking up most of the space on the other side of the fence—but I should remember that Lydia's there, too. And Memama and Grandpops and, I guess, Adam Cooper.

❧

On August 1, I climb back over the fence. I climb the stairs to our apartment as slowly as possible, and I close the door quietly behind me. Mom steps out of the kitchen and holds out her arms, waiting for me to come to her. She looks neither happy nor sad to see me. I don't know what I feel—it's not happiness or sadness. Those words are too simple.

"Hi, Mom," I say.

EPILOGUE
BACK HOME

⌒

The apartment is, well, the apartment. Mom is Mom.

My first night back, I'm sitting alone at the kitchen table. Gloria and Maureen and Jakobe are still out there, and so is Marvin. Both Marvins. Even though I'm staring at a beige wall and not a window, I imagine the shadow of my dinosaur, and, maybe, somewhere along Red Mountain, the light from a bedside table where my old stepdad is reading himself to sleep. I imagine Memama and Grandpops's apartment, with all the little glass statues sparkling. I think of Adam across town, and I wonder if Alexia is working at the gas station tonight.

I think about what Adam said, about how family are the people who stick with you, drool or no drool. The ones who you don't have to try with. Maybe you get two families—the one you're born with and the one you make yourself. The one you choose. Maybe your family can stretch in front of you like a golden spiderweb, going on and on and on.

Maybe you have to help it along, though. Something as fragile as a spiderweb can break if you're not careful.

Mom and Lionel are out doing the grocery shopping, so there's no one home to ask me where I'm going when I slip through the front door and make my way down the stairs. I smooth my hair and tuck in my T-shirt as I walk to Lydia's house—it can't hurt. I knock on the door and wait. Then I knock a second time. I could ring the doorbell, but I think that's more obnoxious somehow. More disruptive. I don't want to make Lydia's mother mad before she even gets to the door.

Finally I hear the dead bolt turn, and the door swings open to show me Lydia's mom. She's drying her hands with a dish towel. Her nails are shiny and red.

"Hi, Mrs. McAllister," I say, since she doesn't say anything.

"Hello, Nell," she says, politely but coolly. "I think Lydia explained to you that I'd rather she not see you anymore. I know that can't have been pleasant to hear, and I'm sorry. But I did mean it. I think it'll be best for both of you to have a little space from each other."

"Yes, ma'am," I say. "I understand. But could I talk to you for a minute, please? I'd just like to try to apologize for my mother."

I can see she didn't expect that. She twists the dish towel in her hands.

"Sweetie," she says, "I think your mother is capable of apologizing for herself. If she had any interest in doing that."

I want to be very careful about this next part. I've been thinking about it ever since I came home, every time I look across the yard and see Lydia's house. If I can do this right, there's a chance that I could get back life with Lydia the way it used to be. But first I have to make her mom listen.

"Mrs. McAllister, I know my mom should be the one apologizing to you," I say. "She's the one who messed up. But you're punishing me for it. So I'd really appreciate it if you'd give me one chance to try to fix it. That seems fair. I think. Just one minute to talk to you."

For a second, I think she'll slam the door. If I had to guess, I'd say she thinks my little speech was: a) true, and b) annoying. But she stands back and lets me in.

"I don't mean to be unkind to you, Nell," she says. "You're a nice girl. But I do believe that your mom is a bad influence, and I don't want Lydia around her. And it would be nice for both of you to make new friends."

"I am sorry for whatever my mom did or said," I say. "I'm extremely sorry. And that's part of what I wanted to say to you. And I totally agree with you about making new friends. I've made some new ones, and they're great. But they're not the same as Lydia. Please think about letting me and Lydia still be friends. I'll take out your trash for a year or give Saban baths or any other punishment you like. Just don't make me stay away from Lydia."

She shakes her head. "Nell . . ."

I interrupt her, because I need to say a little more. Not to argue with her—arguing will get me nowhere. I have no strategy, no devious plan—all I'm doing is asking her to give me a chance. And then it's up to her.

"I know my mother hurt your feelings," I say. "But I'm not my mother. It wasn't easy for me to come over here and knock on your door and say all this. I only did it because nobody in the world means more to me than Lydia. That ought to matter. It ought to count for more than my mother. Please."

I watch her face very carefully—her lipstick is perfect, and each eyelash is curled—and I can tell that she's considering what I said. And she's feeling something, although I can't tell what. Frustration? Discomfort? Guilt? Sympathy? I hope it's sympathy. But I don't say anything else. I keep looking at her, even though it would be much easier to look away, because I'm hoping she can see how much I mean what I'm saying.

"I don't want Lydia to come over to your apartment," she says finally.

"Okay," I say, hoping.

"But you're right," she says. "You're not your mother. And it was very mature of you to come over here and have this conversation. I appreciate that. You're welcome to come back over here. Just like always."

I hug her. Really tight, and I probably wrinkle her perfect shirt. I've never hugged Mrs. McAllister before, but she doesn't seem to mind. She pats my head, and I feel the damp dish towel brush against my neck.

"You want to go up to her room now?" she asks.

"Yes, ma'am."

I can't stay long because Mom and Lionel will be back anytime, and they'll wonder where I went. But I stay long enough to bounce a little on Lydia's squishy bed and roll around on her furry carpet. We throw a ball for Saban and try to make him bring it back to us. It's stupid, but I almost get choked up while we're playing fetch. When I had Lodema, losing Lydia's house didn't seem quite as important. But as I let Saban lick my face, and I see the glow-in-the-dark stars on the ceiling, all I can think about is how much I need this. Lydia's room feels more like home to me than my own bedroom. No one yells at me, I never feel like I should lock the door, and, let's face it, she has much cooler stuff than I do.

I can't let my spiderweb shrink down to the size of my own apartment—it has to keep spreading. The wider it reaches, the stronger it gets.

"I'm glad you're my family," I say to Lydia.

"I'm glad, too," she says, spinning around in her zebra chair. "It's nice to have you sitting here in my room again."

When I get back the apartment building, I see Lionel's car, and I rush up the stairs. But apparently no one was too worried about me. The apartment is completely still and quiet when I open the door. There's a thin beam of light from the lamp to the sofa, and it falls on Mom's kneecap. She's asleep. I guess Lionel is asleep by himself in their bed. I tiptoe toward the couch and study Mom's face. I'm not sure I've noticed the lines around her eyes before. She's frowning as she dreams. I pull the blanket from the arm of the sofa and spread it over her. Her bare feet are pale and small and somehow sad. I tuck them under the blanket.

Then I walk to my room and lay my hands on the cool glass of the window. No stars tonight. Just the lights of the city. They stretch out as far as I can see, and they make this apartment seem small and unimportant. The lights flicker and flash like a secret code. I don't know what it means, but I know it's a message. I know it's for me, and I know one day I'll decipher it. It makes me think of fences, of a whole world full of fences, and of choosing when you climb over and when you come back. Sometimes you climb and sometimes you wait. For now I watch the lights, and I wonder what comes next.